To the Top!

Adventures of a Small Town Boy

Warren Carlson

ISBN 978-1-954896-66-6 Hardbound

ISBN 978-1-954896-65-9 Paperback

ISBN 978-1-954896-64-2 ebook

Library of Congress Control Number: 2024917396

A shorter version of To the Top was originally published as a Kindle edition in 2015. The author has updated and added more stories to this new edition.

Cover illustration Argeo Jobim

Publisher's Cataloging-in-Publication Data

Names: Carlson, Warren, author.

Title: To the Top! Adventures of a Small Town Boy / Warren Carlson.

Description: Anchorage, AK: Fathom Publishing Company, 2024. | Summary: Jack, a young man growing up in 20th century California, learns about life as he adventures outdoors with his friends and parents. His final goal is to climb Mt. Shasta with his mother.

Identifiers: LCCN: 2024917396 | ISBN: 978-1-954896-66-6 (hardcover) | 978-1-954896-65-9 (paperback) | 978-1-954896-64-2(ebook)

Subjects: LCSH California--History--20th century--Fiction. | Hiking--California--Shasta, Mount (Mountain)--Fiction. | Self-reliance—Fiction. | Friendship--Fiction. | Family--Fiction. | Coming of age--Fiction. | Adventure fiction. | BISAC YOUNG ADULT FICTION / Action & Adventure / General | YOUNG ADULT FICTION / Boys & Men | YOUNG ADULT FICTION / Social Themes / Emotions & Feelings | YOUNG ADULT FICTION / Social Themes / Self-Esteem & Self-Reliance

Classification: LCC PS3603 .A75335 M8 2024 | DDC 813.6--dc23

Printed in the United States of America

warrencarlsonwriter.com | fathompublishing.com

Fathom Publishing Company

P.O. Box 200448 | Anchorage, Alaska 99520-0448

Table of Contents

Acknowledgments

This book is dedicated to my late wife, Lucille Nichols, whose unwavering support of me as a writer and for this book in particular was a major factor in its publication. She also acted as my first "editor" and proof reader. I miss our spirited discussions of what to put in and what to leave out. She was a woman much loved and admired.

Both *To the Top! Adventures of a Small Town Boy* and *A Boy A Bike Alaska!* are books celebrating people of good will in my life and the power of neighborhood. Many of Jack's adventures in *To the Top!* are based on my experience growing up in a small New England college town and helping to raise two boys in a small Oregon college town.

Being a writer is an adventure that started for me when my fourth grade teacher read a short story of mine to the class. I decided right then that I wanted to be a writer.

Special thanks to Connie Taylor and Fathom Publishing for keeping me on track during the preparing for publication part of the journey.

Chapter One
Fire in the Canyon

Twice that hot summer day, my friends Trevor, Davie, and I ran for our lives from the fire in Grave Creek Canyon. The first time we panicked and abandoned our fire line when the wind shifted and the fire rushed at us through the brush. Our crew boss, swearing like a sailor, chased us back. We fought and held the line. The second time we ran when the fire "crowned out," the tops of the pine trees exploding in flames and the wind pushing the inferno toward us!

We ran and the fire ran with us. The burning wind singed our ears! It sounded like a jet plane was about to land on top of us. My legs ran in that heavy dream-like way. We ran together like ghosts through the smoke. My shirt felt like it would melt onto my back. I needed oxygen but the smoke-filled air was burning my lungs. I ran with just one thought—to reach the beaver pond at the bottom of the ridge. We ran like fear-crazed deer.

Buffeted by the smoke-filled wind created by the firestorm, we stumbled down the muddy bank of the pond and dove into the shallow water just as the very worst of the firestorm reached us. We stayed underwater as long as we could. The fire made a crazy orange pattern on the surface of the water. We came up for air slapping the smoke away then swam underwater to a large boulder in the center of the pond. On the far side of the boulder, we surfaced. It was easier to breathe. Soon, the heat and smoke passed away. We were alive!

"I can't believe we did this," Trevor said, laughing. "Jack, you made it seem so real. Maybe you should be a writer someday."

"Next time," Davie added, "maybe we can dive into a clear lake instead of a scummy beaver pond."

"There won't be a next time," Trevor said. "Next time it will be some other crazy adventure."

"Only with you in charge, Jack, would we go for a hike in the woods and end up filthy and wet with all our clothes on," said Davie.

"It was good practice. We might fight fires together some day," I answered.

"One for all, all for one," we pledged before leaving the pond.

"We can't go home like this," Trevor said. "We must smell terrible. Jack, my friend, it's all your fault. You read all those adventure books and then you talk us into acting them out."

"Most fun I've had all week," said Davie.

"There's a small creek a hundred yards that way," I said.

We washed our clothes and ourselves as best we could. We hung our clothes on tree limbs to dry and lay in the sun happy with the world, happy to be growing up in a small California town. In another month we would all be starting eighth grade together. My summer was filled with mowing lawns, helping my dad on weekend construction projects, skateboarding and spending time at our tree house in the woods and, of course, reading. I can go anywhere in a book.

That evening, in a hammock slung between two trees in the far backyard, while my father, William, sat on the back steps improvising on his guitar, I finished the book I was reading about the Tillamook Burn.

In the 1930s, this giant Oregon wildfire produced whirlwinds that tore trees out by their roots and sent mushroom shaped clouds of smoke thirty thousand feet into the sky. Burning branches fell on boats fifty miles off the Oregon coast. Smoke turned day into night. Chickens came home to roost in the middle of the day.

* * *

The following morning at the breakfast table, I was still thinking about what it was really like to fight a forest fire. Would I be brave enough?

"Jack. Are you going to eat those pancakes before they get cold?" my mother, Irene, demanded. I poured on some real maple syrup and dug in. My father was outside smoking his first cigarette of the day and watering our garden.

"Do you have lawns to mow?" Mom asked. "The Jackson's yard is looking a little ragged."

"I'll do it and the Anderson's."

"And the breakfast dishes."

"And I have baseball practice. I'll be fine."

"Your lunch is in the fridge."

My father tapped on the window and waved good-bye as he walked down the driveway next to the house. My mother blew him a kiss. He waved again and got in his truck to go to work as a carpenter. My mother worked at the front desk in a dry cleaner's and hoped to start attending community college in the fall. She wanted to work as a legal secretary.

"I'll be home by six. We'll go out for pizza," she said.

"Okay."

"Don't skip lunch."

"Okay."

Neither of us said anything for a minute. It was a game we played. I knew what she was going to say and I knew she was reluctant to say it.

"What?" I said.

"You know I hate to ask you, but check on Mrs. Monahan, please."

"Okay, Mom."

"It's our Christian duty."

"Okay."

"I have to go."

"Okay."

She hooked her long brown hair behind her left ear and leaned over and kissed me on the top of my head. I concentrated on my pancakes and pretended not to notice. I guess I liked it but I was glad she never kissed me in front of my friends.

The house always seemed too quiet after my parents left for work. I missed them. I like spending time with them. My parents are young. They got married when my mom was sixteen and my dad was eighteen. Before washing the dishes, I decided to go to the backyard and read just one chapter of my new book, a sea adventure called *Two Years Before the Mast* by Richard Dana.

When my parents bought the house three years ago after living in a double wide trailer, the backyard was a mixture of abandoned flower beds, dead grass, and bare dirt. Dad hauled in topsoil and planted grass. He liked taking care of it. I never had to mow it.

Trevor lives in the house just behind us. Years ago, we nailed boards on both sides of the wood fence to make climbing over it easier. You never knew when one of us might appear in the other's yard. This morning, while I embarked on my sea adventure, I could hear Trevor practicing his violin. One hour every day. It wasn't an unpleasant sound. In the afternoon, he spends an hour with his French tutor. Even so, he's an okay guy. He said to me once when I teased him about not being athletic, "Sports may be important to you now but when you graduate, they won't matter. Being academic and musical will matter."

After I finished the first chapter of my book, I took a minute to listen to the sounds of the neighborhood: a car passing, a dog barking, a screen door slamming, Trevor's younger twin sisters playing some game in their backyard, a bad-running lawn mower making choking sounds and, unfortunately, our next-door neighbor Mrs. Monahan, singing along with a Christmas album with the volume turned up high. This was something she did at least twice every summer. At Christmas she plays old rock and roll records with her living room window facing us wide open! Once I saw her dancing in the front yard. It was one of the few times I saw her looking happy.

I went back inside, washed the dishes and sang along with Mrs. Monahan's record which was loud enough for me to follow. Checking on Mrs. Monahan was the chore I hated the most. My mother said that she "had problems" but I knew she was completely nuts. I had seen her walk an imaginary dog right down the street, holding on tight to a leash even though it trailed behind her. A few times she had sprayed my father with a garden hose while he was barbecuing in the backyard. About once a month, in good weather, she would lie down on her front lawn and pretend to be dead. Neighbors ignored her. The first stranger coming by would call 9-1-1. When she heard the sirens, she would jump up and hide in her house.

The job of checking on Mrs. Monahan had fallen to me by default. If my mother went over, Mrs. Monahan would go on forever about her sister's drinking and her son not caring about her. If my dad went over, she would flirt with him—I didn't want to think what that was like—and invite him for a beer no matter what time of day it was. When I knocked on her door, she usually answered it, but I never knew how she would be dressed. In winter she usually answered wearing pajamas and a robe that looked about a hundred years old. In summer she answered in her gardening outfit: yellow shorts and a Hawaiian shirt, straw hat, and huge sunglasses. For a week last May she appeared in a long, sparkling thing which I guessed was an evening dress.

Every morning, I would say, "Good morning, Mrs. Monahan, how are you today?"

And she would say, "You're a good boy, Jack," and close the door.

I would breathe a sigh of relief and get on with my day. If I added anything to my greeting like "have a nice day," she would get agitated. She was a short, stout woman who spent day after day shoveling in her garden. My mother said she would plant something in one place then move it over and over again. She seemed, as my father would say, "tightly wound." I suspected she was far stronger than people realized. If she didn't answer the front door, I was required to go around the back corner of her house to see if she was working in the garden. I was not allowed to go any farther. She would stop shoveling and walk toward me as if I was an intruder. Then she would figure out who I was and we would have our morning "conversation." I admit it. I'm afraid of her and her shovel. I didn't like turning my back on her to walk away.

This morning, already muggy and warm, she answered the door dressed in a wool shirt, wool pants with suspenders and a logger's hard hat; clothes that her late husband, a logger, must have left behind. I was glad she wasn't carrying an axe! Instead of stopping on her side of the screen door, as she usually did, and looking around me at the street to see if it was safe, she banged the door open and charged out. I jumped aside. She stood at the top of the porch steps blocking my escape. Hands on hips, she looked up and down the street, perhaps deciding if it was a good day to be a logger. It gave me the willies.

I recited my usual speech to the back of her head without any real hope that she would answer me, but she turned around and said as always, "You're a good boy, Jack." But as she said it, she stared intently at a rusted lawn chair that had been on the porch winter and summer for as long as I could remember. I had never seen Mrs. Monahan sitting in it. I remember seeing her husband there smoking a cigar. Was she seeing the ghost of her late husband? Just then I remembered that his name was also Jack. The thought made the hair stand up on the back of my head.

"I have lawns to mow," I managed to stammer as I took two steps, placed a hand on the porch railing and vaulted onto the lawn, just clearing a bed of geraniums.

Chapter Two
Time for a Swim

When I returned from baseball practice that afternoon my dad was in the street unloading a small backhoe from a trailer. He had the biggest grin I had seen on his face in a long time.

"What's the backhoe for?" I yelled over the growl of the diesel engine. My father just waved while looking over his shoulder as he guided the backhoe down the metal ramps attached to the back of the trailer. When he had it safely on level ground, he turned the motor to idle.

"Jack, my son, we are going to build a swimming pool. The boss let me take this home but I have to return it to the rental place by six."

I nodded, wondering if he had gone a little nutty. He loved our backyard and now he was going to dig up part of it for a swimming pool? It was a big backyard but still...

"It's awfully narrow between the house and the fence," my father said, breaking into my thoughts. "You watch the fence side and I'll keep track of how close I am on the house side."

Dad drove slowly forward. When he reached the back corner of the house, he had to make a turn without hitting the garage. He inched the machine forward and back three times before slipping through. He turned the machine off and looked at his lawn. Was he having second thoughts?

"We're going to dig a hole two feet deep, eight feet wide, and eighteen feet long. Then we'll build a wooden box around it two feet high and line it with plastic. And there you have it, the world's cheapest swimming pool. It will be shallow but that way no one can drown."

"It sounds great, but won't it need water?"

"Wise guy. I bought a submersible pump. We fill the pool

7

with the garden hose. Once a week we pump it back out on the lawn. No chlorine."

"I guess that is thinking, in this case, inside the box, but why?"

"You deserve it. You're a good son. After you graduate from high school in five years, I can re-do the lawn. Also, I thought if I swim after work it might help me to quit smoking."

"That sounds great."

"Let's get working. We'll use the dirt from the hole to build some BMX jumps next to the back fence."

"Make one tall enough and I can jump the fence into Trevor's back yard."

"Err, I don't think so."

"Dad, I can't believe it. You're the greatest!"

"Enough of that. We're two men with work to do. Climb up and hold on tight."

I stood behind him and held on to the back of his seat. He expertly peeled back the turf where the pool was going to be and pushed it into a pile.

"Mr. Jones down the street is going to come over with a wheelbarrow and haul it away to redo part of his lawn," Dad yelled to me over the roar of the engine.

"Is the pool going to cost a lot?" I asked. I was worried because I had heard my parents argue about money and the fact that neither of them could balance a check book. He pretended not to hear me.

After Dad cleared the space for the pool, I climbed off the backhoe and, using the tape measure, checked the size of the hole as he continued to work. I watched carefully as he moved the levers that first extended the arm, then dropped it so the teeth on the bucket could dig in. Next, he pulled back on two levers at the same time, so the bucket and the arm curled together until the bucket was full of dirt and above ground. I thought it looked like a giant arm and hand reaching out, palm down, to scoop up the dirt.

When the hole was about three quarters done, my father called me over.

"You have been watching me work the levers, haven't you, Jack?"

"Yes sir! It looks like fun."

"It is," he answered, laughing. "It's like having the strongest arm in the world. Come on up and give it a try."

"Really?"

"Yes, just don't tell your mother."

I sat on my dad's lap. That way he could take over if something went wrong. I lifted the bucket off the dirt pile and swung it over to the pool area. Slowly. The bucket seemed to pick up speed on its own as it passed over where I was supposed to dig. I pulled back on a lever and the arm came to a sudden stop, shaking the machine. Now I was nervous. It was harder than it looked.

"Slow, but not too slow. Steady," my father said.

I took a deep breath, held it, exhaled. "Concentrate," I said to myself. "It's like being at bat in baseball. You have to pay attention." I swung the arm to the left, opened the bucket and dropped the teeth into the ground.

"Good, son. Now just think of the arm and the bucket as an extension of you. You are going to curl the bucket into the ground and at the same time bring the arm back to you..."

I almost did it. My dig was too shallow, so I came away with just a half bucket of dirt. I did swing the arm smoothly and added the dirt to the pile. Out of the corner of my eye I saw my father looking at his watch.

"You're doing fine. Now each time increase the speed a bit."

I lost myself in the work the way I sometimes lose myself in a book, blocking out everything else, even the outstanding fact that my father and I were building a swimming pool. I was briefly distracted by the idea that perhaps he hadn't told my mother. As I worked, my father said very little. He was very good at not being a "helicopter parent." However, I talked to myself while operating the controls: "lift it now, more angle, oh, too much, bring it in, now swing to the right."

After about twenty minutes, Dad said I had done a good job but told me to get off and take some measurements. He trimmed the hole here and there and fine-tuned the bottom. It was fun to watch him. When he was satisfied, he used the bigger bucket on the front of the machine to change the pile of dirt into three BMX jumps. I helped him maneuver the machine past the garage and down the driveway to the street and load it on the trailer. We had just enough time to return it to the rental shop before it closed. On the way home, we stopped for milkshakes. "What a great day!"

We pulled into the drive behind my mother's car. Neither of us got out.

"How are you going to pay for it, Dad?"

"Remember the big fight your mom and I had when I bought that rifle last summer?"

"Yes. I never heard her yell like that before."

"I sold it to a gun collector for twice what I paid for it. And I'm not going to pay for it all by myself. You're going to help me."

"How?" I asked, picturing mowing about fifty lawns a week and shoveling endless miles of sidewalks in the winter.

"Saturday morning concrete," he answered.

I could guess what that was about, but I asked anyway.

"I'll explain later. Time to face your mom."

"Is the hole in the backyard going to surprise her?" I asked fearfully.

"Well, we talked about it. At the beginning of summer. But today, when the backhoe was available free, I figured what the heck."

"I think I'll wait here until the yelling is over with."

"Don't worry. She'll be won over when I tell her about selling the rifle and my two handguns—she never liked having guns in the house—and my plan to quit smoking."

"Good luck, Dad."

"Thanks. Now come on. We're in this together."

"Okay. You gave up your guns and let me drive the backhoe so we're partners."

We found her sitting in a lawn chair on the back porch drinking an iced tea and staring at the hole in the yard.

"I'm sitting here, and I am asking myself, what is it? And

what happened to the grass? It looks like the outline of a very shallow swimming pool. I go to work and when I come home, I expect the house and the yard to look the same as when I left in the morning. Is that too much to ask?"

"Let me explain," began my dad.

I bolted. I ran across the lawn, yelling back over my shoulder that I had to see Trevor about a book he borrowed, and I was over the fence before they really noticed I was gone. I knocked on Trevor's door and he joined me outside. We sat on a tall double swing set that was there when his parents bought the house ten years ago. (Earlier in the summer Davie had launched off the swing at its height and done a perfect back flip. Trevor and I had declined to follow his example.) Worried that Mom would turn down the project, I pictured filling in the hole using shovels. I couldn't hear any shouting. My dad must have convinced my mom that the pool wouldn't strain our budget.

"Jack, when you build the pool, I want to help," said Trevor.

"Thanks, come over after dinner and we'll try out the jumps."

"Okay."

From the back porch my dad yelled out, "Jack? The coast is clear—"

"Not really, not completely, but let's go for pizza," Mom added.

We drove to the pizza parlor. For some reason I felt like they were on a date and I was tagging along. To my relief they had their usual end of the day conversation. While we waited for our pizza, we had salads and Dad explained "Saturday concrete."

"The boss gets calls for small concrete jobs he can't be bothered with. So I thought Jack and I could build the forms Friday evening and pour the concrete on Saturdays."

"Do you need a permit?"

"For small, non-structural jobs, no one will care. There's good money in it. It will pay for the liner, the pump and maybe a filter system."

"William, you work hard as it is."

"I'll be fine. It's important... well, I don't really know why it's important but it is. I want to do this. A family project."

"Can I invite the girls over for a pool party?" my mother asked.

"Of course, anytime."

I couldn't tell if they were serious. "Mom, he did sell his guns. We dug the hole for free. I want to do this."

"Well, it takes a lot of water. How long will it take to fill? I know you're good at math."

"Twenty-four hours to fill. Twenty-four hours to empty," Dad answered.

"Are you guessing?"

"No. I figured the cubic feet, converted to gallons then timed how long it took to fill a five-gallon bucket."

Looking at Dad, my mother said, in a teasing way that signaled to me that the battle of the swimming pool was over, "You're smarter than you look! Do you promise to swim laps while I float in an inner tube and egg you on? And quit smoking?" she added under her breath.

"No. The pool will be too short for laps but I figure I can anchor a bicycle inner tube to one end, hook my feet in it and swim. Don't tell me to jog instead. I don't mind feeling foolish in my own yard but not out in public. Besides women whistle at me."

"There must be a lot of desperate women out there."

"Enough, my wonderful wife. Do we have a deal or not?"

We all said "deal" and fist bumped.

"That is still a lot of water. Maybe I'll pay for a filter if that would help."

"That would be great Mom," I said. "Love you, guys."

Chapter Three
Pay the Piper

We didn't talk much the rest of meal. We had agreed to take on a big project. Things could go wrong. My dad tried to be reassuring.

"It will be okay, Irene."

"It better be. I can't tell if this is one your better ideas or the opposite."

"I won't let him operate any power tools."

"Mrs. Monahan told me that you let him run the backhoe."

"I really should cover up that knothole in the fence. I promise he will come home with all ten of his fingers."

"And his toes?"

"Yes, Irene."

"How many of these Saturday jobs will it take to pay for the pool?"

"Five or six. The money from the guns will pay for about half."

"Can I help or is it a guy thing?"

"Something like that."

When we drove down our street, Mrs. Monahan was lying on her front lawn pretending to be dead.

"William. You should check on her just in case."

"All right."

We pulled into our driveway. My father went next door. As soon as he opened the front gate Mrs. Monahan jumped up and ran inside. We sat on the front porch to have our ice cream. Mrs. Monahan came back out but when she saw us, she ducked back inside. Just another day on our quiet street!

After dessert, we went back inside.

"Our first job is Saturday. Here's what we will be doing,"

Dad said as he showed me a drawing of a curving sidewalk and a small pad for a storage shed. He explained to me about scale. On construction drawings, to make the plans small enough to fit on a piece of paper, a quarter inch on the paper stands for a foot in...well, real life. Otherwise, the plans would have to be as big as the project. That would never work. I could see I was going to learn a lot. I hoped I would be able to work hard enough to please my dad.

I like to work, I really do. School's okay but you don't get paid and most of the time you're not doing anything except sitting still and listening. I have trouble sitting still. I asked the teacher if I could go outside occasionally and run around the building a few times. She thought I was joking. On top of all that sitting, my mother insists that I get all A's and B's. She dropped out of high school to marry my dad and had to go back to get her G.E.D.

Chapter Four
Trevor Questions

The next evening after dinner my parents went to the movies, a sure sign that all was well between them. I decided to ride my bike over to Davie's place to tell him about the pool. Over the two years we had been friends, I had worked out the fastest way to get to the trailer court where Davie lived with his dad. He was a quiet man. He worked as a machinist, bowled in the winter, and fished in the summer. He was a good cook, a skill he was passing on to Davie.

From my house I rode to a city park, then followed a dirt track next to the railroad tracks. Sometimes a train would come by. The noise, the wind, the vibrations were unnerving. Mt. Shasta was turning golden in the setting sun.

I crossed the tracks on a dirt road bordered by some commercial green houses and a long-abandoned trailer that winter snows had flattened. I cut through a vacant lot and headed down an alley that ran by some of the older houses. Both Davie and I liked this alley because people threw away good stuff like old radios that were fun to take apart, bicycle parts, magazines (some my parents wouldn't approve of), pieces of metal that might be useful someday. This evening, I found a fishing pole with a damaged reel that I was sure Davie could fix. My parents didn't want me to bring things home but Davie's dad didn't mind and loaned us tools to fix things.

When I reached Davie's place, he was sitting on the front porch peeling the bark off a forked tree branch to make a sling shot. I gave him the reel and sat down next to my friend and told him about the pool and Saturday morning concrete.

"Our first job is Saturday."

"The pool sounds great," Davie said, "and I found the perfect tree to build a tree fort in—a real fort, a real tree, not something in a book."

"Yea. Yea."

"I was hoping we could get together with Trevor on Saturday."

"Can't be helped. Where will we get the wood?"

"There's an abandoned pile of wood in back of the old sawmill."

"Where's the tree?" I asked.

"On the far side of Ford's creek. It's perfect. I bet we'll be able to see Mt. Shasta, the river, and the big snag from up top."

The snag was home to a golden eagle nest. That spring, with binoculars, we had watched two eaglets take their first flights. It would be great to be able to see into the nest. What we called "our" woods was really a large tract of land on the far side of the interstate once owned by a lumber company but now forgotten.

It was bordered by the highway, a country road, and the golf course. We had never seen anyone else there. There were short cliffs to climb, an old dump where we shot BB guns, a rope swing, logging roads to explore on our bikes, and a small shack we had built the summer before on a ledge halfway up a hundred-foot cliff; a shack we told our parents about or maybe they found out and then we told them. No fires during fire season was the rule. We cooked meals on a small camp stove. We had conversations there that we didn't have anywhere else. We were a gang of three.

Davie was the job foreman on all our building projects. He was a year older than Trevor and me. He had to repeat fifth grade after missing most of the school year. While his parents were divorcing, his mother took him on a long road trip to visit relatives. They were country folk and Davie had spent the time helping with farm work. He returned with a collection of tools and the confidence he could build anything he could find the materials for.

Using an old logging road, we could get from Davie's trailer to the shack in fifteen minutes on our bikes. Sometimes we rode there after dinner to hang out and watch the evening light on Mt. Shasta. The mountain is over fourteen thousand feet high. Sometimes we saw ventricular clouds over the summit that looked like spaceships. Often, just before sunset (and time to head home) it would glow with what was called "alpenglow." People sometimes died on the mountain, mostly from falling rocks or an uncontrolled descent. This fact did not discourage us from believing we would climb it someday as a team.

The shack was eight by ten feet with a weather-tight sheet metal roof and a deck. For furniture we had two lawn chairs Davie had found in the alley by his trailer and patched with duct tape and a bench made from an old car seat. Our shack overlooked a beaver pond fed by a small stream that appeared and disappeared in the marshy ground. Trevor always brought a pair of binoculars once owned by his grandfather. One time we watched a mother beaver teaching her kit how to make repairs on a dam. Trevor was into birds. He knew the names of many and could identify them by their calls.

We never told any other friends about our shack. It was mostly a place to go and talk about people we knew, especially people we didn't understand. s. He would sometimes tell us the news. (Was anything outside of our home town important?) Often, we only pretended to be interested. We did talk about our dreams. We took our dreams seriously. We hoped, I guess, that would help them come true. That summer before eighth grade I dreamed of playing center field for the Dodgers, skiing in Switzerland, being a smoke jumper, climbing Mt. Everest, and reading every adventure book in the library.

Davie wanted to save money all through school, buy a motorcycle and the day after graduation, ride to New Orleans and get a job on an oil platform for five years, then return to Mt. Shasta City with enough money to go partners with his dad to buy a house. Trevor planned to go to college in France, play the violin in an orchestra there, and then return to the United States for medical school.

Trevor is cataloging all the life forms in the meadow below our shack. He is making drawings of all the plants and listing all the birds. And he asks us questions that are hard to answer. And he says things like, "I like riding my bike because it is mechanically efficient, unlike skateboards." His parents have allowed him to turn their garage (they paid for a heating system) into a combination greenhouse and science lab. He has a collection of dead birds he has stuffed. He does chemistry experiments.

Last summer he made gun powder then made a rocket out of a cardboard tube from a clothes hanger. When he launched it, the rocket went over the side fence, just missing the neighbor's dog as the dog's owner was looking out her kitchen window; the same dog that Trevor trained not to dig in his mother's roses by burying an electrically-wired piece of aluminum foil just under the dirt and waiting for the dog to do his mischief. When the dog peed on the rose bush the electrical current traveled up the urine stream. The dog took off like a missile—howling! From then on, every time the dog came up the street, he crossed over when he got to Trevor's house! Trevor's parents ended his rocket career but never told the dog's owners (not the most popular people).

Late last fall, on our last trip to the shack before winter, as we stood around a trash barrel fire, Trevor suddenly exclaimed, "And, there is ice!"

"What's so special about ice?" I asked.

"It expands, I mean when water turns to ice it expands. That means—"

"I know what expands means," Davie interrupted. "But what's the big deal. Water freezes. We skate on it. It melts and we swim in it. What else do we need to know?"

"It floats. Think about it. Even though it's a solid, it's lighter than water, a liquid, which is pretty weird. Think about what would happen if ice was heavier than water."

"I'd rather think about girls or skateboarding or food—"

"It would sink to the bottom," said Trevor. "And then the next layer would freeze, and then, Jack, what?"

"Hmm. Pop quiz. I guess the rivers would freeze solid and that would be really inconvenient. How do you come up with these ideas?"

"It's easy. Almost automatic. I come across a fact then I think about it and guess what would happen if it changed."

"Maybe you should write science fiction?" Davie said sarcastically.

"And what about water itself?" Trevor said, ignoring Davie.

"Don't ask," Davie said to me.

"Think about it," Trevor continued. "Each water molecule is made up of two hydrogen atoms and one oxygen atom."

"Tell us something we don't know," said Davie.

"Atoms that are holding on to each other just right—"

"I know a girl I would like to hold onto just right," said Davie.

"So the water can flow. If they let go, the atoms would fly apart and then all life would die off and if they held on tighter rivers would flow like molasses!"

"Finally," Davie said. "We're talking about something important—food. Our wonderful Frosty Freeze is closing today for the winter. Let's head back to town for a last giant order of fries. My treat."

As we hiked down the cliff to where we left our bikes, I heard Trevor say to Davie, "Have you ever wondered how water gets to the top of a tree?"

* * *

All that happened almost a year ago. We're still friends, Trevor is still a mad scientist. The Friday before my first Saturday concrete job with Dad, I was helping Davie fix the fishing reel I'd found while we talked about money; about how we needed money to make our dreams come true; about the mystery that some people, who seemed no smarter than others, were rich. Davie showed me his savings book.

"There's over four hundred dollars here!" I exclaimed. "You couldn't have saved that much just helping at your uncle's grocery store."

"See that green trailer over there? That's Mr. Stevens. He's retired from the railroad. He spends most of his time reading. He can't drive and uses a walker so he pays me to go to the library for him."

"I know you do errands for people but still—"

"And the Airstream? Miss Cindy. Her sister visits every Friday for cocktails. The only trouble is, Miss Cindy is a terrible housekeeper. Every Thursday I help her clean up. And the blue and white at the end? Mr. Oberson. His hands shake too much to write his letters to the editor, even on a keyboard. I've seen him try and I've heard words come out of his mouth that even my dad never uses."

"I've seen some of those letters. Pretty out there."

"I'm just the scribe. There are others."

"Even so, fifty cents here or there. I mean, Davie, four hundred dollars!"

"They all overpay me."

"Why?" I asked.

"I think it's because … I'm not sure if this is right, I've thought about it. I think it's because I don't judge them. And unlike a relative, I like, you know, helping them. And talking to them. They have good stories that are new to me. Mr. Stevens was once a race car driver. He showed me photos. He pays me two dollars every time I go to the library for him. I'm sitting on a gold mine here in this dumpy trailer park."

Just then Trevor rode up on his bike. Davie gave me a hand signal not to mention his business dealings. Trevor didn't have money issues. His parents had decided he didn't have time to work and gave him a generous allowance. Trevor's mom sells real estate, and his dad teaches biology at the community college and works at a research lab that moved up from San Francisco. Both of them are on schedules so irregular Trevor never knows when they will be home. They opened a charge account at the corner grocery and the Frosty Freeze for him and he has been teaching himself to cook. "I just think of cooking as a chemistry experiment."

Davie came back with, "Don't invite me over for dinner any time soon."

"What were you guys talking about? Something I'm not supposed to know?"

I didn't know what to say but I wasn't surprised by Trevor's question. He is very observant. Davie went back to a conversation we had earlier. A subject he knew more about than me, or so he said. Girls. And what we looked like to them and other stupid questions.

"Our friend Jack is having a going into eighth grade identity crisis."

"No, not really. The whole question of me, us, and girls—it's upsetting."

"Do you need a tissue for your issue?" said Trevor then realized how dumb it sounded.

"Sorry. We're friends. Let's talk about it."

"Okay. Do you think I'm ordinary? Looking, I mean? I

look in the mirror and I could be anyone—I don't mean someone else, just that there isn't anything special that I can see."

"True. Absolutely ordinary. You could be anyone," said Trevor.

"Boring," added Davie. "I'm surprised we even recognize you day to day."

"I'm surprised you recognize yourself in the mirror," Trevor added.

"Come on guys. I'm serious. I'm not tall like you, Trevor, or all muscles like Davie."

Ignoring me and speaking to Davie, Trevor said, "Or as mature as you—"

"That's an unfair comparison, he's a year older."

Ignoring me again, Trevor continued. "He does have that space between his teeth and blue eyes. Ariel told me she thought he was cute."

"Really?" I asked.

"Maybe that's what she said. She giggles while she talks, makes it hard to understand her."

"Or take her seriously," said Davie. "Besides, is cute a good thing?"

"Maybe. Maybe not. But Jack, I have seen her look at you with 'come to me' eyes," said Trevor.

This was too much. We all burst out laughing.

"There must be something special about him," Trevor continued, speaking to Davie.

"He's a loyal friend, a born leader, plays a great center field and his parents are cool," Davie responded.

"Thanks," I said. "I'm sitting right here. No need to talk in the invisible third person."

"Trevor. See? He made a clever observation."

"Whatever. I need to be home in ten minutes to check on one of my experiments. I'll see you guys tomorrow." As he rode away, he said, "Jack, it's okay to be ordinary."

"Thanks weirdo," I called after him.

Chapter Five
Saturday Morning Concrete

The first concrete job Dad and I did together was that Friday evening. It was a patio slab behind a house on Maple Street. After he got home from work, and before Mom returned from her job, we made ourselves some sandwiches. I felt like we were teammates getting ready for a big game. On the ride over, Dad detailed the four principles of construction: plumb, level, straight, and square.

"Plumb, if you are building a house, means all the walls are vertical. You check using a level. Straight? We use a complicated tool; a piece of string just like carpenters have done for hundreds of years. Level: for concrete work we'll use a transit. My boss is letting me take it home on weekends. You'll see how it works. And for square we will be using some of that geometry you learned last year. You got an 'A,' didn't you?"

"Yea, I did."

"Your mother and I are pleased with how hard you work at school, and well … just for being a good son. It's great when we get to do things together. I love you, Jack."

Hearing Dad say that surprised me. And I realized it wasn't just kind words. I realized that he really, really meant it. We pulled into the driveway. For some reason, I waited until he was about to get out before saying, "I love you too, Dad."

He paused and nodded his head. Time for the team to get to work.

There was no way to get equipment into the back yard without cutting down a prized maple tree which was out of the question. Shovel time. We cleared an eight by twelve area using a pickaxe and shovels. We dug down eight inches and piled the dirt behind a tool shed in the back yard. Then Dad made trip after trip with a wheelbarrow to move a pile of gravel from the drive to our excavation. My job was to rake the gravel smooth to make a good bed for the concrete.

Next, we used boards to build a box that was the same size as the future patio. A rectangle has opposite sides the same length. You can determine if the four corners are all ninety degrees by measuring from corner to corner on the diagonal. If it's square, the two measurements will be the same. The corner-to-corner idea on paper in geometry class works in the real world too. Corner to corner divides the rectangle into two right triangles. I held the "dumb end" of the tape at one corner while Dad pulled the tape to the opposite corner and noted the measurement. We did it again for the other corners.

The measurements were slightly different, so we moved one corner in a little and one out and the diagonals measured the same which meant all the corners were ninety degrees. I wasn't sure if I really understood it or was just saying yes to please my dad. He drew a sketch on a piece of wood. It looked just like an illustration in my math book. I got it. Math in the real world! Next, we pounded in wooden stakes around our box. Using the transit, we made sure the box was level. This was something new to me. "Level is when a marble set down on the middle of a floor doesn't roll anywhere. But, in this case, to make sure the concrete pad will be level we take a "shot" or "reading" with the transit on all four corners. The readings have to be the same.

Dad set up the transit on a tripod and leveled it using two little knobs. Now anything that matched the line inside the transit would be level. I held a rod with a built-in ruler on the first corner. "Five feet, and ten and a half inches," Dad called out. I went to the second corner. It was a half an inch lower. We lifted the board and nailed it to a stake. We checked the next two corners and made adjustments until all readings were the same which meant our pad would be level and square. I felt good about using math in the real world. By the time we finished it was eight at night, we were under attack by mosquitoes, and my hands, despite wearing gloves, felt blistered. I did feel proud about how hard we worked and a little sad thinking about how hard my dad worked all the time.

On the way home, Dad, satisfied that he had taught me something, said, "Yup, using math you can build a house ..."

"Plumb, level, square and straight," I responded.

"That people can live in. Use math to build a boat and sail away."

"Use math to build a rocket to send it into outer space."

We were two tired but happy campers.

When we got home Mom was waiting for us with meatloaf and apple pie and ice cream for dessert.

"I've been trying to keep it warm. It might be a little dried out," she added with a hint of criticism for how long we had worked. Dad and I ate like old time lumberjacks, slowly and silently, too tired to talk.

* * *

The next morning, we were at the jobsite at eight. We waited for the concrete truck to arrive. I could tell Dad wanted to smoke a cigarette but he tried never to smoke in front of me. His smoking was one of the few conflicts between my parents even though Mom had given up nagging him. I guess quitting isn't easy. Everyone he worked with smoked.

We heard the concrete truck coming up the hill. It pulled in front of the house and backed up the driveway. The big barrel was spinning slowly. The concrete in the barrel rumbled, the gravel in the mix rattled against the metal sides of the barrel. With a whistle of escaping air, the driver set the brakes and climbed down from the high cab. Instead of the burly guy I expected, the driver was a slightly built blond woman about thirty-five, with a bright smile and friendly handshake for me.

"You must be Jack. I'm Barbara. Your dad said you would be helping out. Having fun?"

"I like working with him."

"If you work as hard as he does on every job, you'll be okay."

Barbara pulled down on a lever at the control panel and the barrel revolved faster. She and Dad listened.

"Sounds a little dry," Dad said.

Barbara pulled a lever to add more water. They listened again. I could hear the difference. They decided it was just right. Barbara lifted heavy metal troughs from their storage racks behind the cab of the truck and fitted them together to form a chute for the concrete to slide down. Dad positioned a wheelbarrow at the end of the chute. Barbara pulled down on a lever and concrete rushed down the chute. She cut off the flow just as the wheelbarrow was full. Dad wheeled it away and I maneuvered a second wheelbarrow under the chute. Barbara filled it. Before I could even think of trying to wheel it away, Dad was back to take it away to dump it in our forms.

When our forms were almost full, Dad stopped and looked at the revolving barrel of the concrete truck with a worried expression on his face. He and Barbara listened.

"How much do you think is left?" he asked.

Barbara climbed lightly up the metal ladder and looked into the still revolving barrel. "About a quarter of a yard."

"That should just make it."

Dad explained to me that if he had ordered more than he needed, he would be paying for concrete he couldn't use. And if he ordered too little, he would have to rush to the lumber yard to buy sacks of dry mix concrete we would have to hand mix with water to finish filling the form. It would cost us money we hadn't planned on spending. We watched the concrete fall slowly into the chute. The concrete ended when the wheelbarrow was almost full.

"That should be enough," Dad said.

But he looked afraid that it wasn't. I followed him to the backyard. It was just enough! In a tired voice, he said to me, "Welcome to 'Saturday Morning Concrete,' Jack."

"Thanks. I'm glad to be here."

"Now we have to smooth it out before it hardens. I'll stop by tomorrow to remove the form boards and pick up our first paycheck. We did okay money wise. After we finish, let's stop for donuts and take a look at the mountain."

I had discovered there was a great view of Mt. Shasta from a vacant lot on the hill above the railroad yard. Once in a while my dad and I would stop for a visit with "our" mountain and talk about stuff. Mt. Shasta was part of the reason our family lived here. On their honeymoon trip from Los Angeles to Oregon, Mom and Dad had stopped overnight in Mt. Shasta City and driven to the base of the mountain on a full moon night. Dad had trouble believing it still had snow on it in July. They decided that Mt. Shasta City would be a good place to raise a family.

Mt. Shasta is a stand-alone volcano. It isn't active but maybe it is just sleeping. It has two peaks. The highest is 14,180 feet above sea level and about 10,000 feet above Mt. Shasta City. Sometimes only the peak is seen above the clouds. In winter, on clear and windy days, plumes of blowing snow tell me the world up there is wild. I've wanted to climb Mt. Shasta ever since Doctor Ballard, an adventurer who lives down the street and has climbed Shasta eleven times, loaned me a children's book about mountain climbing in the Swiss alps. I daydream about standing on the summit and looking down on my world. Three or four times a summer my family does a picnic hike in the wildflower meadows below snow line. The sky is so blue! The air so clean. The water in the small creeks so cold!

Mt. Shasta is sacred to Native Americans, a mecca to western mountain climbers and a magnet to spiritual seekers and what Dad calls "mountain nuts." Some believe the mountain has healing powers. Others, that it is a landing site for UFO'S and the home of Lemurians, a magical race of beings who hollowed out the mountain with sacred bells. (Yes, bells!) In the old days, people claimed they were sometimes seen away from the mountain. They were easy to spot because of their tall heads. My father joked that they could blend in by wearing ten-gallon cowboy hats. Others believed that just living next to the mountain was enough to change people for the better. Maybe, maybe not. I love living next to Mt. Shasta. It feels special.

So, on the way home from the concrete pour, we stopped at Dad's Donuts for two maple bars, a cup of coffee and an orange juice. We parked facing the mountain. It looked a little hazy, not as crystal clear as on a brittle, cold winter day.

"Have you saved enough for a ski pass?" Dad asked me.

"Just about …"

"Something on your mind?"

"Girls."

"Uh-oh. I guess I should have given you—"

" 'The talk?' Don't worry, Trevor has filled me in."

"Trevor? I guess I'm not surprised."

"His father told him and he told me and we looked at some of his father's human physiology books. It seems pretty straight forward, the physical part."

"Really? Then what?"

"Last year at school, there were some couples. They held hands in the hall. Kids talked about them and then the next week they wouldn't be speaking to each other! What I need to know is what are girls all about, as, I don't know … people?"

"That may be the hardest question you have ever asked me."

"Do you want me to ask Trevor instead?" I said, feeling sort of angry. "You're my dad, you're supposed to know things!"

"No, no, the question just took me surprise. They are all different, girls, women, no two alike. Personalities are what I'm talking about. Your mother and her sister, raised in the same house, different personalities."

"I'll say. Aunt Kathy is too hyper for me."

"Do you have a possible girlfriend in mind?"

"No. Not really. I'm just trying to figure out the rules of the game."

"Philosophers, psychiatrists, novelists have been trying to do that for centuries."

"Do you have any advice at all?" I asked, feeling desperate.

"Yes. Since there are no two alike, take the time to get to know them as individuals."

"How?"

"It can be hard. If I remember junior high correctly, everyone was trying their best, well, not to be individuals, to be like everyone else. That, and the girls never seemed to be alone, they walked around in clumps. Does that sound about right?"

"Yes. Talking non-stop."

"Are any of them as nice as your mother?"

"I don't know. I've been going to school with some of them for years but, I don't know, I don't feel that I really know them. Sometimes they seem mean to each other …"

"Competition, I guess. You and your friends compete. Tease each other?"

"But we aren't mean about it."

"Here's my advice. When you meet a girl you like, if

everything she says is important to you, if you care about who she is ... what other students might think isn't important."

"Are you telling me not to listen to my friends?"

"Yes."

"Maybe just Trevor? He's a genius, isn't he?

"It seems that way. I hope it works out for him."

"What do you mean?"

"The world isn't always kind to people who are different."

"Trevor, Davie and I all have different personalities but we're a team."

"I'm glad they're your friends."

"It's not fair, is it, the world?"

"The world?"

"Some people have food, a place to live, and love, like us, but others don't have any love in their lives."

"Are you thinking of Mrs. Monahan?"

"Yes. She's hard to figure out."

"Impossible. When we first moved here, shortly after you were born and her husband was still alive, she was more normal. I know she is hard to be around, but we need to be as kind to her as we can."

"We need to be of 'good character?'"

"Yes."

I thought about how difficult that would be. It was one of those times when growing up looked about as hard as climbing the mountain.

"Dad, do you think we could hike up to Lake Helen this summer? We talked about doing it last summer." Lake Helen, at 10,000 feet, is the jumping off place for summit climbs.

"I'm not a little kid anymore so I don't really believe you can see San Francisco from there like you said, but I just want to be higher on the mountain, maybe talk to some climbers."

"Well, Jack," he answered, talking slower than usual. "I don't think I could do it. My lungs aren't in good shape. I've cut down to six or eight cigarettes a day, but still, all those years of heavy smoking." He took a sip of his coffee and looked at the mountain.

I'd almost forgotten that he smoked. He smoked at work but

not at home. He would walk around the neighborhood for a last smoke of the day. Sometimes I smelled it on his clothes.

"I'm a smoker and that's all there is to it. Maybe you and your mother could go and tell me all about it."

"It's okay. Maybe someday you'll finish a pack and then just not buy another one."

"It could happen," my dad said but he didn't sound hopeful. He finished his coffee and started the truck.

"We'll stop at the lumber yard on the way home, pick up the boards and plywood we need to build a box around the hole we dug, then line it with plastic and, voila! a swimming pool. We'll work on it after church tomorrow."

"The three of us are going to church? You usually sleep in."

"Keeping peace with your mom. We made a deal: Saturday concrete, Sunday church."

Nobody asked me, I thought to myself but wisely didn't say anything out loud. We usually went to church just once a month. "I was going to go fishing at Canyon Park with Trevor and Davie."

"Not going to happen. Besides, you probably do more rock climbing than fishing out there. It worries me some."

I tried again. "I thought church would be like watching the stars or being on a mountain. Inspiring somehow. The sermons are confusing." My father didn't answer.

I knew that, in church, my mother felt the mystery of it all. I guessed that she celebrated life differently than my father did. Thoughts like this made me feel that I still had a lot of work to do to understand my family and myself. My mother has a good singing voice ("as long as you don't ask too much of it," she would say) and if my father follows her lead, he does all right. I pretend, afraid that my changing voice will crack and people will notice.

God is a subject I thought about a lot that summer. So many questions. It was mostly the stars that made me think about really big questions. At the beginning of summer, Trevor and I climbed up on the roof of their garage with his telescope and looked at the universe. Of course, Trevor knew the names of most of the constellations but somehow that didn't make them any more real to me.

Millions and millions of stars. How could it be? Millions of galaxies filled with millions of stars so far away that it took the light from those stars, traveling at 186,000 miles a second, years to reach me, an insignificant boy on the roof of a garage in a small town in Northern California. How could my brain, or anybody's brain, even Einstein's, take it all in?

And closer to home, there was the mountain, 600,000 years old, right there in my backyard. It last erupted 800 years ago. My science teacher told me that in geological time that is like yesterday. And what about all the life in a drop of water looked at under a microscope? If God made everything, where did he get the raw materials? I admit, many of these questions came partly from talks with Trevor, but I thought about it on my own and talked about things with Davie who pointed out how much we don't know about the people we live with right here in Mt. Shasta City.

* * *

The swimming pool was a hit. My friends and I strung a net across the pool and played one-on-one volleyball. We built a launch ramp and running full speed did mid-air skateboard type moves. And, when my parents weren't looking, front flips! When Dad got home from work, he would change into a bathing suit and float around in the pool on an inner tube. Mom twice invited girlfriends over for an "iced tea social (men not allowed)." They wore fancy hats and pretended they had joined the country club. We emptied the pool the day after school started.

Chapter Six
For the Love of the Game

It hurts to get hit by a baseball. Some pitchers in our summer baseball league lack control. After being hit three times early in the season, fear made it hard to concentrate. I was embarrassed. I wasn't helping my team the way I wanted to. I love the game, how it all makes sense. There is nothing to figure out except how fast a runner is—would he try to stretch a double into a triple? I love the sound of the wooden bat meeting the ball. I can usually tell from the first few feet of trajectory where the ball is going. Last week, I fielded a short fly ball bare handed on the first bounce and unleashed the throw of a lifetime while the runner was casually trotting down the base path assuming he had a hit. When my throw arrived at first base two steps ahead of him, he stopped, totally confused as to where the ball came from. Still confused, he looked out to center field. I waved. The umpire called him out. The opposing coach started to protest, then went back to the dugout. It took a few seconds for the hometown fans to figure out what had happened. Scattered applause. I thought at the time that throw would be something I would remember for a long time.

Before the beginning of the season, I bought a new glove. I loved its clean leather smell. For the first two weeks I kept it tied up with a ball in it to form a pocket and slept with it next to my pillow. That glove and I were having a good season. Four times, so far, I had chased down long fly balls: running, running, running even though it seemed impossible, then the ball falling into my glove softly, like a bird. The distant cheering of the crowd as I held up my glove in triumph!

I started the season batting sixth. In our last game, I

batted ninth. Mostly I hit ground balls up the middle which are fielded easily by the pitcher or second baseman. I was only getting on base one out of five times. The situation was made worse by a new kid named Norton. He just moved here a few weeks ago. The bad news for me is that he can hit. He substituted for our right fielder when he was out of town for two weeks. Norton batted four hundred with one base clearing double.

I had started for every team I had been on since I was seven years old. Was that about to end? I thought about how embarrassed my parents would be if they came to a game and I was riding the bench. I could imagine my father having words with the coach. I found him in the swimming pool floating on an inner tube.

"Dad. About the game on Thursday? I don't know if I'll be starting or not."

"Not starting?" my father said. "Have you been skipping practice?"

"Of course not." I explained to him about Norton.

"Well, you're right, he did hit well the last two games. Jack, my son, don't despair, I have an idea."

"But you have to talk it over with Mom?"

"Have some faith. She has money and a list of groceries for you to buy for Mrs. Monahan. I told her you would shop for her. She doesn't ask for help often. When you get back, we'll talk."

"I can't see what you can do, you can't bat for me," I muttered as I walked back to the house. When I got back with the groceries, Mrs. Monahan, looking like she hadn't slept in a week, pointed to the kitchen and held the door open for me to deposit the groceries. As I was leaving, she pressed a quarter into my hand and held on for an extra moment. It was creepy but I guess I could feel how lonely she was.

My parents were on the back porch. My dad was smiling. My mother was making a grocery list and talking out loud, listing the items. "We're doing a big shopping trip across the border to Medford, Oregon," my father announced.

I almost told him I didn't want to go but I was curious why he was smiling. He hated shopping.

"While your mother is shopping, we're going to spend an hour at that batting cage place."

"As if that will help."

"Attitude, Jack, attitude. Here's the good news. I called a high school baseball coach I happen to know and he's agreed to meet us there. I signed us up for an hour. He's going to spend thirty minutes with you."

"Wow! That's … sorry about the attitude."

* * *

"Jack, this is Coach Wilson."

"Pleased to meet you, sir. Thanks for helping out."

"Step in there and be a hitter. Try not to think about how to swing, just watch the ball. Matter of fact, first ten pitches, don't swing at all. But let's see your stance."

I remembered to lift the bat above my shoulder. I watched the ball. I had read that major leaguers, when they were batting well, could see the stitching on the ball.

"Imagine you can see the stitching on the ball," Coach Wilson called out. "Okay, swing at the next five pitches."

I hit one solid line drive.

"Are you afraid of the ball?" Coach Wilson asked.

I was tempted to lie but he already knew the answer. "Yes," I said.

To my surprise, he said, "I was too, when I was playing. Your swing is okay but you don't look determined to hit. Picture hitting a line drive to left field and try to see the bat meet the ball. In other words, don't just swing, imagine a powerful swing connecting."

Ten swings and three line drives later, I felt it was working. There is that certain sound of the bat meeting the ball that says you are on target.

"Keep going," Coach Wilson called out. "It's just you and the ball, try to let everything else disappear. You don't need to see the rest of the field out of the corner of your eye. And a final thought, don't feel rushed. You're an experienced baseball player. You have all the time you need."

I could feel it when my concentration was enough and

when it was not. I did my best to stop thinking. I could feel the change.

Coach Wilson called me over. "You're doing fine. Your dad's going to buy a half dozen balls and pitch to you after dinner most nights."

"Thank you very much, sir."

"You're welcome. Good luck."

I batted for another twenty-five minutes, feeling more competent by the minute. My arms got tired. Dad stepped in. I turned up the speed on the pitching machine. He still had it. I was proud of him.

* * *

We picked up Mom at the grocery store and headed back to California. She didn't ask me about batting practice. I could tell she was building up to one of her do the right thing speeches.

"Whether you start the game on Tuesday or not—"

"At practice on Monday, I'll prove to coach I can hit. I'm looking forward to it."

"Don't interrupt."

"I'm sorry," I said. I knew I was skating on thin ice; I just wasn't sure why. I leaned forward a little and looked at my dad. He glanced out the window.

"If you start or not, you have already learned some things."

My mind raced before I answered but I couldn't think what things. "It must really suck to ride the bench."

"And?" my mother prompted.

Why was she torturing me? "If I can convince Coach to start me, I will have overcome adversity," I said, feeling hopeful I had discovered at last the lesson she was trying to teach me. I swear I could see my dad smiling. *Did he enjoy seeing me instead of himself on the hot seat?* I stayed silent. Maybe I hoped my parents would talk about the price of groceries (cheaper in Oregon) or something else. No such luck.

"I want you to think of this situation from Coach's point of view."

I confess. I had no idea what she was talking about. "What?" was all I could manage. My mom didn't say anything. To me, Coach was just Coach. He had been a baseball coach forever. He lived across the street from the field. His kitchen sometimes acted as a first aid station. He raked and lined the infield. I got it. I pictured Coach sitting at his kitchen table, drinking a cup of coffee and looking at a list of starting players and trying to decide if he should cross my name off. "Well, maybe it is hard for him, sometimes, to be a coach. I'll just have to hit really well at practice!"

"Exactly," my father said.

Then Mom said, "I know there's a league rule that everyone has to play at least three innings. No matter how well you hit in practice, I want you to go to coach and volunteer to sit out the first four innings."

"You're kidding," my dad said with some anger.

"Not at all. This is an excellent learning opportunity."

Both my father and I mouthed the words "learning opportunity." My mother was always finding "learning opportunities" like helping Mrs. Monahan or mowing a small lawn down the street that belonged to a blind lady for free. It was practically a hobby with her. She saw us mouthing the words.

"Careful," she said in a tone of voice that would strike fear in the heart of any twelve-year-old. I was stuck.

Even if I played great at practice, I would still have to talk to Coach. My mom was sure to check on me. "All right, Mom. Whatever you say." I didn't expect my dad to interfere. I stared out the window the rest of the way home. Even the first view of Mt. Shasta didn't cheer me up.

Chapter Seven
Honesty is the Best Policy

When we pulled into our driveway, Norton was sitting on our front porch. There was a glove, bat, and a canvas bag on the lawn next to his bike. He came over to our car and introduced himself to my parents, then helped carry in the groceries. I showed Norton the swimming pool, because whatever we were going to talk about, I wanted it to be away from my parents. I told him about "Saturday morning concrete."

"You and your dad working together, that's great. My dad and I used to do things together in Anaheim before he moved to Alaska. He'll be back. We moved here because it's cheaper."

"Anaheim? Isn't that where Disneyland is?"

"Yeah. My mother worked there. We got some free tickets. After a while it's boring. I'd rather go down a real river or climb a real mountain."

"I'm going to climb Shasta someday."

"Maybe I—"

"Let's get through the baseball season before we even—"

"Right. Jack, I came by for a reason. I don't like playing outfield. Unlike you, I never seem to quite know where the ball is going. I want to pitch and you need batting practice."

"I just spent an hour at the batting cage in Medford."

"That's great but it's not the same. The machine didn't hit you with any pitches, did it?"

"Boy. Does everyone know I'm afraid of the ball?"

"It doesn't hurt that much."

"Fine."

"Here's the deal. My dad used to pitch extra practice to me. There are ten balls in the bag."

"My dad just bought a half dozen."

"Great. We can go to the high school field. I'll pitch and you hit."

"Okay."

My mother came to the back porch and invited Norton to have dinner with us. He accepted. I told them about our plans. My dad looked disappointed. Our meal was quiet. It kind of felt like Norton wasn't comfortable talking to adults. We agreed to meet late the next morning after my mowing jobs.

"I'm glad you're making friends with Norton but it doesn't let you off the hook about talking to Coach," Mom said after Norton left.

The next day, on the way to our special practice, we stopped at the bike and skateboard shop to look at the new dirt bikes. As we were leaving, Norton said, "Just a second, I forgot to ask the guy something."

When we got to the park, I saw Norton slip a plastic bag with two foot pegs in it out of his shirt and drop them into the ball bag. *I bet he stole them.* The clerk had been talking on the phone with his back to the door when we left. I thought I should say something to Norton, but I hardly knew him. *Maybe he had paid for them. He was in and out of the store in seconds. He must have stolen them.* I decided to think about it later, maybe ask my dad's advice.

I had an old catcher's mitt that had been my uncle's. It was large for me. I tightened the lacing and put it back on. Norton picked up the bag of balls and went to the pitcher's mound. I squatted down behind the plate. Norton could throw hard but lacked control. Some pitches hit the dirt in front of the plate. I was glad I had a large catcher's mitt to protect myself. I had always played outfield and wasn't used to digging balls out of the dirt.

I called time out. "Look, Norton, you're throwing too hard. How about this, just look at my glove when you throw. Don't worry about speed."

"I like throwing hard."

"You look angry. And it's not working."

"Whatever."

"Coach doesn't tolerate wild pitches. He gets irritated

whenever our pitchers walk someone. It's like giving the other team free base runners."

"And the game goes on forever. Okay. I'll give it a try."

It worked. Almost none of the pitches were wild. I relaxed a little. We stuck with it for another twenty minutes, then called it a day and decided to meet again in the morning when I would take a turn at bat now that Norton had more control. I worried over whether I should tell my parents about Norton and the foot pegs.

When I got home, my parents were still at work. I jumped in our homemade pool to cool off. After splashing around and seeing how long I could hold my breath under water, I decided to practice my swimming. I hooked my feet in the bike inner tube Dad had nailed to the end of the pool and, held back by the inner tube, I did a lazy breaststroke. The cold water felt good on my sore shoulder muscles. After I cooled off, I joined my dad on the back porch. He was playing his guitar and sipping on the one beer a day my mom allowed him.

"I think Norton might have stolen something."

"From here? Before we got home from shopping?"

"No. From the bike shop. Foot pegs." I told him the whole story.

"Maybe he ordered them earlier, forgot to pick them up, went back inside."

"When we first went in, the clerk wasn't on the phone. Why didn't Norton ask for them right away? Besides, if he ordered them special ..."

"He would have bragged about them."

"That's how I'm thinking," I said wearily.

"Put it aside for now. I'll talk to your mother."

I had trouble going to sleep. I wondered what would happen if I told Coach about Norton shoplifting instead of volunteering to let Norton start the game. Even having this thought bothered me. It was what my mother would call an "ignoble thought." I knew I wasn't going to be a tattletale but still I felt like it ... just for thinking ... I finally went to sleep by imagining one perfect single after another.

At breakfast the next morning, my mother informed me

that she had called Norton's mother and they were meeting for coffee.

"I'm a snitch."

"You did the right thing."

"I'm going to pay."

Two hours later while I was mowing Dr. Ballard's lawn, my mother pulled up to the curb. I turned off the mower and went over to her.

"You worry too much, Jack. It went well. Since his father left, Norton has been impulsively stealing, perhaps things he imagines his father might have bought him. His mother searched his room and found the pegs and some other things from the bike shop. All unopened. He has to return them and apologize."

"I hope the store owner doesn't think I had anything to do with it."

"Norton told his mother it was all his idea."

"I still feel like a snitch."

"Let it go. You worry too much. I have some good news."

"Okay," I said, a little worried about what it might be.

"My high school transcript came in the mail today, mostly A's, so I stopped by the community college and picked up an application, I'm sure I'll get in. I'm hoping to go part-time in the fall and take care of you, your dad, the house—now might be a good time for you to learn how to cook!"

"That would be okay, I guess. Trevor says it's like doing a chemistry experiment."

"We'll talk again later."

With that she drove off and I went back to mowing the lawn. After I finished, I met Norton again for our private pitching and batting practice. I rode by the skateboard shop without stopping. Practice went well. We both worked, didn't talk much.

That evening, I got to the team practice early. I helped Coach haul equipment from his garage across the street from the ball field.

"I need to talk to you," I said. Coach grunted in reply.

"My m—that is…It must be hard to be a coach sometimes."

Another grunt. We reached the dugout and dropped the equipment bags.

"I think Norton and I should share—he's a great hitter—center field, or something, to be fair."

"Ummm...Your mother told you to say this?"

"Yes."

"I'm still impressed. However, I just got a call. Ted's grandfather is seriously ill. Ted will be gone the rest of this week, maybe next week. Norton will take his place in right field."

"But Ted's our best hitter."

"Can't be helped. Norton will bat third. And here's a surprise. I've decided you're a better hitter than you believe you are so I'm moving you up to sixth in the batting order but only if you promise not to try for home runs. You don't have the power."

"I promise," I answered wondering if my dad had anything to do with this, if he had bragged to coach about my hitting at the batting cage in Medford. I decided not to ask.

"If Ted gets back next week, then center field will go to you or Norton, whoever plays best this week."

"What's best for the team?" I said.

"Exactly!" said Coach as if I had hit a home run.

"I've been helping Norton with his pitching, and he's been pitching me batting practice."

"He hasn't said anything to me about pitching. I'll let him throw some tonight."

I fell asleep that night thinking about baseball and "doing the right thing" and woke up thinking about Christmas.

Chapter Eight
Christmas in July

On the first weekend in July, I woke to the voice of Nat King Cole singing Christmas songs. I felt confused as I went to my bedroom window half expecting to see Mr. Cole himself standing there when I raised the shade. Instead, there was Mrs. Monahan, dressed in a purple dressing gown with an orange feather collar, using a stick to prop open the firewood door next to the chimney so we could share her joy for Christmas music playing on her record player. I guessed the speakers were pointed at the firewood door. She went back inside and turned the volume up to near the crackling point. It was a "joy" she would share with her neighbors almost continuously for the next three days from six a.m. to ten p.m.

Mr. Cole's rich, sincere, and beautiful voice filled the quiet summer morning. Mom came in from the kitchen and stood with me at the window. "Well, this is an unusual way to start a summer morning," she said, laughing. It would be the last time she laughed for days.

"How long can she stand it?" my mom asked. The answer turned out to be long enough to summon one old friend, her nephew, two ministers (who apparently were afraid to confront her individually), one social worker, and eventually a policeman, all of whom tried to persuade her to turn down the volume. She pretended she couldn't hear them. She would answer the door dressed in her late husband's lumber jack outfit. I wondered if some responders had the same thought I did, that she had an axe just inside the door, out of sight.

"Let's have breakfast, Jack. Your dad already left for work."

"Will he talk to her when he gets home?"

"You mean if the music is still going? You know I don't like him talking to her."

"You're not going to make me—"

"Of course not."

I wondered what Mrs. Monahan could possibly be doing while the music was so loud.

"I'll be right back." I jumped up and ran into our backyard and did a chin up to look over the fence.

Returning to the table, I said, "She's not in her yard."

I pictured her dancing, maybe holding the axe, but then I realized most Christmas songs might be hard to dance to. Next, I imagined her cooking breakfast or even reading a book, completely unbothered by the music. Maybe her messed up mind allowed her to block out the real world. Maybe her mind had a mind of its own. I saw her in a kind of trance watching the record go around, around, around ... gathering her evil powers.

"Are you all right?" Mom's voice cut in.

"I'm fine. Just thinking about baseball."

"I have to get ready for work. Your lunch is in the fridge."

"I think I'll mow my two lawns earlier than usual. After that, well, Trevor asked me to help with an experiment."

"Hopefully nothing involving gun powder or electrocuting dogs."

"No. I promise. Maybe when I get back it will be July again instead of December. If not, I wonder if Trevor might have any ideas."

"Don't want to think about that possibility."

"Just kidding."

"What is it? I know something is on your mind."

"Mom ... about going to college, aren't you a little old?"

"It's a community college, not Harvard or Stanford."

"Still ..."

"Other people are going to be thinking that maybe, so what?"

"I love you, Mom."

"I love you too," she said, giving me a hug.

"About Mrs. Monahan? Do I have to check on her today?"

"You can skip it. We'll assume she's alive."

"What if she plays Christmas music forever?"

"I don't know. Maybe the needle will wear out. It must be awfully loud in there."

After my mother left, I stood on the front porch and sipped my orange juice. Across the street Mrs. Keegan was on her front porch. We acknowledged each other with a half wave and a "what is this all about" gesture. *Silent Night* came on, a Christmas song I could sing. I decided to mow lawns instead.

We had a game that night at seven, but Coach had agreed to meet Norton and me at four for extra practice. Me for hitting and Norton for fielding. He wasn't happy about playing right field instead of pitching, but he didn't have the control our regular pitchers had—a pitcher who threw a lot of balls made for a slow game. As we played catch and waited for Coach, Norton asked how I could tell where the ball was going as soon as it came off the player's bat. "I'm not sure. I guess I watch the swing and listen to the sound of the hit. If you pay attention, it's easy to tell how well it is hit. Then the angle of the ball tells me which way to run."

"Sounds easy enough. At least I'm not stuck at first base which I played in my old town. I hated fielding ground balls. You never know how they will bounce."

Coach showed up with two bats and a bag of balls. He paced off the distance from the mound to the plate starting five feet in front of the backstop. For a target, he hung a catcher's mitt on the backstop. I jogged out to the outfield. Norton stepped in to bat. He hit well but mostly to left field. "With runners on base, I want you to hit behind them, to right field and don't try for a home run. At your age, possible home runs are fly balls that get caught, making a long out."

Norton did okay. Then he said something foolish. "Come on, Coach, show me your best pitch." Coach had played in college as a pitcher. The ball zipped past Norton as he feebly waved at it with his bat. When it hit the catcher's mitt, it made a loud smacking sound and the glove fell off the wire. "I changed my mind," said Norton. "Don't show me your best pitch."

We laughed.

"Jack's turn," said Coach.

"With Coach pitching, I wasn't afraid of the ball. I felt I

was batting as well as Norton. I almost lost my concentration when I briefly fantasized about us winning our next three games and the league championship.

"Eyes on the ball," Coach called out.

"Show me your best pitch." I started my swing just as he released his fast ball. I saw the ball, I saw my bat hit the ball, I saw it sail out to short right field, a solid hit. I don't know which of us was more surprised!

"Let's end batting practice on that," Coach said.

We moved to the outfield. He hit fly ball after fly ball to us in rapid succession. He ran us ragged.

"That's it, boys. I have a good feeling about tonight's game."

As we were leaving the field, Norton's mother, a tall red head wearing a nurse's uniform, got out of her car and walked over to Coach. Norton and I held back.

"She's thanking him for giving me a second chance."

"Second chance?"

"Don't play dumb with me. Coach could have kicked me off the team for stealing. My mother made me confess to him."

"That must have been hard."

"I don't know why I do it—steal. Sometimes I just throw the stuff away."

Chapter Nine
Baseball but Still Christmas

I could hear Mrs. Monahan's stereo as soon as I turned the corner at the end of our block. My mother and several neighbors were standing on the lawn across from her house. I dropped my bike on our lawn and went over to join the group. Al and Kathy Johnson are both retired forest service employees. Three or four times a summer they get together with my parents for a barbecue. They travel a lot and have the calm, steady look of people who have spent much of their lives in the woods. I loved hearing about their backpacking trips and foreign travels.

They were talking with Janet Nottingham who works part time as a social worker and Mrs. Singer, a widow who lives on the other side of our house. The music ended abruptly with a terrible screeching sound as Mrs. Monahan apparently dragged the needle across the Silent Night record. She then cranked up the volume to what must have been the maximum. It rattled the windows. I half expected everyone to flee.

"Maybe I should go talk to her," Mrs. Nottingham said. She marched across the street, through the gate, up the walk and onto the porch without breaking stride. Then she hesitated. The music stopped. We could see Mrs. Monahan come to the screen door and say something. Then the door closed and Mrs. Nottingham, looking shell shocked, came down the walk and turned right without closing the gate or saying anything to her supporters.

We held our breath. The silence continued. I could hear cars on the next street over, birds, and even a lawn sprinkler. Was the neighborhood drama over? My mother looked disappointed. Sometimes I think she wants drama to happen. I said to her, "I think I'll go for a swim."

"While it's quiet?"

"Yes."

"I'm going to the store. Your dad will be home soon. No front flips."

"I think I'll follow Dad's idea and swim with my feet hooked in the inner tube."

"It's working, the exercise. He's smoking less, not coughing as much."

"That's great."

"Maybe we can go to the lake this weekend."

"Sounds good. Can Davie go with us? I haven't seen him much lately."

"Sure, why not? What about Trevor?"

"He's going to a science camp."

"I heard Davie is working in the back room at his uncle's machine shop even though he is underage?"

"Yes. He's not near any machines. He cleans up, runs errands. He and his dad need the money. The transmission on their truck went out. His dad has been riding Davie's bike to work."

"I guess it's not any of my business."

"How do you find out these things?"

"I work at a dry cleaner's, people talk. Do you want anything from the store?"

"A six pack of coke?"

"Poison. I'll mix up some iced tea instead."

* * *

Okay, maybe it isn't a real pool like the one in Doctor Ballard's back yard, which is long enough to swim laps, but on a hot day the cold water feels great. What would it be like to swim in the Olympics? Great! But think about the hundreds of hours of swimming laps. Years and years of back and forth in chlorine-treated water. My mother would never allow it! I like to imagine doing things. It's a little like reading a book where I can go anywhere and do anything. I like to just think about things. Even in our small town there are always things going on. I read the local paper every day.

After I got tired of swimming, I floated on my back and thought about something real: about going into the eighth grade. My last year as a kid. How much had changed since first grade! My day dreaming was interrupted by ... *Jingle Bells.*

As an experiment, I let myself sink to the bottom of the pool. Wonderful silence but I could only hold my breath so long. I went into the house. Mom and dad arrived home at the same time. I saw them talking in the driveway. Then my mom kissed him on the cheek and pointed at Mrs. Monahan's house. Dad had that "I'm going to kick butt" look on his face but I didn't believe it. My dad is not a tough guy. I joined my mother to see what would happen. He knocked and he yelled. No one came to the door. The music played on. He checked her backyard before coming back.

"If the music is still playing when we get home from the ball game, I'll call her minister. I do feel sorry for her but enough is enough," my mother said.

"Let this be a lesson for you, Jack," my mother added. My father and I looked at each other.

"I have no idea what you mean," I said.

"Sorry. I'm tired."

"You can take a nap at the ballgame." My parents would sit in lawn chairs down the third base line. "I'll wake you up when Jack is at bat."

"How is your batting going?" my mother asked.

"Good."

"And Norton?"

"Okay."

"It must be hard for him, coming to a new town—"

"Please," my father interrupted, "not tonight. We already have Mrs. Monahan on our minds."

My mother stayed silent, but she didn't look happy about it. We finished eating and left for the ball field.

Baseball. The only thing I don't like about it is when I let down the team. It's a lonely walk back to the bench when you strike out in a close game. Coach always says something like "Don't worry about it, you'll get a hit next time." But I do worry about failing, about disappointing my dad. According to my Uncle Pete, Dad was a really good player in high school. I didn't do anything embarrassing and we won the game easily. Norton and I both batted well. I told Norton about Mrs. Monahan. His answer surprised me. "She's mentally ill. Just think how hard it is to be her." Sometimes

I get the feeling that everyone around me is smarter or nicer than me.

When we got back from the game, Christmas music was still playing but not loud. After a dessert of apple pie and ice cream, the three of us sat around the living room and read. It was one of our favorite things to do. My mother likes murder mysteries. She would call out, "I know who did it." Half the time she would be wrong and complain the author had tricked her. My dad is into American history, especially the civil war or "the war of northern aggression" as the authors of his books call it. I like adventure stories. That summer I read books about big game hunting in Africa and gold mining in Alaska.

I kept falling asleep. Finally, I headed off to bed. It was still warm, so I left my bedroom window open. Mrs. Monahan's music wasn't real loud but loud enough. I couldn't figure out how NOT to be annoyed. It was time for a sneak attack. It was dark.

I put on dark clothing. Crouching and keeping to the shadows, I reached the side of her house safely. I removed the stick holding the firewood door open and gently closed the door. The music was muted. Judging from the last few days, when the arm on her record player got to the end of the song, it would play it over again. I only needed a short time of relative quiet to get to sleep. It worked. I slept until morning and woke up to *Little Drummer Boy*. I looked out my window. The firewood door was still closed. I went out on our front porch. Her front door was open. A couple returning from the tennis courts down the street were looking at her house. Easy for them to laugh.

I could hear faint singing. It was Mrs. Monahan. Unlike her mind, her voice was clear. Right then, standing on my front porch, on an ordinary summer day, for the first time I felt truly sorry for her. For an adult. In the past, I have felt sorry for starving children on the news or maybe for a classmate that was bullied but I don't remember feeling sorry for any adult. Adults are free to do what they want! I felt more sorry for her and less sorry for myself for having to listen to her music. I considered going next door and asking her how she was feeling. I thought about her living alone; without anyone to talk to.

If she talks to herself, does it make sense? Does she know she is crazy? Who decides? I almost get lost in some books I read in my fantasies, but I know they aren't real. Mom told me that the neighbors think she belongs in a hospital. They have been talking with her nephew, her only relative.

I stood on our front porch and for a moment, I wished I was as smart as Trevor because I had a new thought. Or a new half thought. A half thought that TIME had something to do with her being one way and the world being different. I go through my days, even lazy summer days, aware of time passing. It's important that we all agree on what time means. It's important that, if dinner is at six, we all know what that means. But if Mrs. Monahan was now completely lost in her Christmas music, her imagination, and her memories, then time for her didn't really exist! Perhaps she didn't even know how long she had been playing her records.

I wanted to ask her how she had arrived at such a sad place in her life. If it happened to her. Then … not quite admitting to myself what I was doing, I walked over to her house. The music stopped with a screech. Through the screen door, I could see her in the shadows (her front window curtain had been closed for months) standing next to the record player. She had already seen me, but I knocked anyway. She came to the screen door.

"How are you today, Mrs. Monahan?" I asked.

"You're a good boy, Jack," she said.

She looked frightened. I felt I needed to say something, to help her in some way. I couldn't think of anything. I almost blurted out, "I'm sorry. I can't help you. I'm just a kid." I might have said "I'm sorry" out loud, but I don't think so.

She said, "I know you're stealing mail from my mailbox." And then she closed the door. I guess she felt I had betrayed her. I walked out to the street and checked her box. It was jammed full. I took out the mail and put it on the small table on her front porch.

That evening, when I got home from baseball practice, there was an ambulance in front of Mrs. Monahan's house and a crowd had gathered across the street. My mother was part of the crowd. My father was not.

"Mom! What's happening?"

"Her nephew got a court order to put her in a hospital. He drove up here from San Francisco and found her down at the school playground. She had chased away kids by throwing rocks at them. Her nephew brought her back to the house."

"She's a threat to public safety," added Mrs. Nottingham. "Look, they're bringing her out."

Two attendants walked her down her sidewalk to the street. They held her by the elbows. It looked like they were almost carrying her. When they reached the back of the ambulance, she briefly broke free—just long enough to shake her fist and curse the gathered neighbors. While one of the attendants held her, the other pulled a stretcher out of the vehicle and they strapped her down. When they drove away, a strange thing happened. Everyone in the group except me started clapping. My mom had a look of anger and triumph on her face. I felt embarrassed. I said, "Why are you clapping!?" It just seemed so wrong.

Several people started talked at once, saying things to excuse what they had done. I wasn't listening. I was looking at Mom. I could see her face change. She looked ashamed. She could tell I felt confused by her action, by the group's action. I crossed the street to our house feeling lost. Dad was cooking dinner. Brats and sauerkraut.

"They hauled her away," I said.

"I was watching from the kitchen window. I don't know why everyone clapped," Dad said.

"You sound angry."

"It doesn't seem right, the clapping. Your mother clapping."

"No, it doesn't."

"Mom's always talking about compassion, doing the right thing. I guess I can see why they wanted to applaud but I don't understand why they did. They aren't kids."

We heard my mother's car start up. I looked out the and watched her drive away. "Where's she going, Dad?"

"Don't know … I talked to the nephew. He left me some money, too much really, for you to mow her lawn and take care of her flowers until things get straightened out. And he left us a key so we can check on the house."

"And water her plants."

"Yes. ... By the way we have a Saturday morning concrete job tomorrow."

"And the final game of the season, against Dunsmuir—league championship!"

"I remember. It's a sidewalk from the house to an art studio, then we'll build a roof over it. Between the posts will be planter boxes. I'll have to do the carpentry on my own but I'll knock off in plenty of time. This job and one more and the pool will be paid for."

"You use it a lot. How are you doing with the smoking?"

"Haven't had one for a week."

"I'm never going to smoke."

"If you do, you'll have me to answer to. Let's eat."

"Deal."

My mother came home an hour later. Instead of joining us in the living room after heating up her dinner, she took her meal out to the back porch, giving us the "don't talk to me" look. Later when I was reading myself to sleep, the window open, liking the quiet, she came in and sat on my bed.

"I'm embarrassed for the way I behaved. I apologize for setting a bad example for you."

"Her nephew hired me to mow her lawn. Maybe Mrs. Monahan didn't really notice people clapping."

She leaned over to kiss me goodnight, but I guess she could tell that I really didn't want her to and she backed off. She closed the door, softly, as if she was sneaking out of my room. I put down my book, put my hands behind my head, looked up at the ceiling and thought and thought.

There was a quiet knock on the door. I could tell it was my dad. "I'm awake."

He opened the door and just stood there looking sad. My parents always respected the privacy of my room. "Come in."

"I think we need to talk some more. Your mother is still upset by the way she acted. What are you thinking?"

"Just now. It will sound funny, but I was thinking how strange, not funny, that Mrs. Monahan spends Christmas alone but has this huge collection of Christmas records."

"I'm glad you're sympathetic. As far as your mother is

concerned, we all do things sometimes that we know are wrong but do them anyway."

"Mom would call that giving in to our baser nature.'"

"Yes. I smoke even though I know it's bad for me. Your mother can be overly judgmental. Demanding."

"Mostly in a good way?"

"Yes. Remember when I caught you hitting Bruno with a stick?" Bruno had been my dad's dog since he was sixteen and died when I was five.

"Yes," I answered feeling ashamed all over again. Bruno had dug up a sandcastle I had built in the sandbox in our back yard. I remembered how he had looked at me with sad eyes as if I was crazy.

"Dad, I don't get what you are trying to say, not really."

"I'm not sure, just, I guess, we all make mistakes, and I sure don't want Mrs. Monahan to come between us."

"We have love and she doesn't."

"Right on. I'm glad you are thinking about things. Trying to figure things out. As you get older and read more, you'll come face to face with how complex people are: we love and hate, are fearful, make war, commit crimes, search for love, know true happiness, and fall into despair. When you are older, I'll introduce you to Shakespeare. In the meantime, here's a book you might like by Hemingway: *The Old Man and the Sea*. It's about courage and perseverance."

"I'm glad all this stuff you're talking about is only going to happen one day at a time."

"I'm sorry if I frightened you. Trying to figure out life, I believe, is, I think, an important part of growing up. And you don't always have to agree with your parents."

"Why didn't you go to college? Why work as a carpenter?"

"I like building things. I used to get restless in a classroom. And maybe I shouldn't tell you this but I I learned more from books than from most teachers. I come home and I forget about work. I have my guitar, books, and you and Irene."

"Are you going to cry?" I asked, surprised.

"Gratitude, Jack, gratitude," he said walking to the door.

"Say goodnight to Mom for me," I called out. I went to sleep feeling older than I had in the morning.

Chapter Ten
Champions

We won! League champions! The season was over. I had hoped to be a hero. Both Norton and I had okay games but Joe Smith, our second baseman, played the best game of his life. He fielded a half dozen ground balls including one near second base that looked like a hit. Joe backhanded it and threw the runner out at first, preventing the runner on third from scoring. He batted three for three including a game winning single. We had men on base, Billy on third and Norton on second. Joe hit a long fly ball between left and center field. Could Norton, our slowest runner, score from second?

The left fielder's throw to the cut-off man playing third bounced once. It took an extra second for him to get control of it. Meanwhile Norton had rounded third and was chugging his way home. The cut off man's throw was high and offline. Norton came home with the winning run without having to slide. We mobbed Joe.

After we got untangled, my dad approached. "You played a good game, son."

"Thanks, Dad."

"What's wrong?"

"I know it's a team sport, but I wanted to be a hero at least once this season."

"Your batting improved a bunch. Maybe next year. Let's stop and get a milk shake on the way home."

Chapter Eleven
The Cartographer

When we got home, I climbed over our back fence to visit Trevor. At the side door of the garage, I had to step over Walter, the basset hound, who barely woke up. He was good at just two things, sitting on the couch to look out the window and running away from home. Neither Trevor nor his parents admitted ownership. When Walter did run away, our town is so small someone would always return him.

When I entered the garage, Oscar, the rabbit, thanks to Trevor, had recovered from a broken leg and was sleeping draped over a chair, air from a fan keeping him cool. He sat up straight and looked at me. I didn't pet him. I figured he was a one-person rabbit.

"How's he doing?" I asked. "I see you took the cast off."

"He's doing fine. I taught Oscar to use a litter box or scratch at the door when he wants to go out. Also, I just pat my leg and he jumps up and takes a nap on my lap."

"Aren't basset hounds supposed to go after rabbits? Isn't it in their DNA or something?" I asked.

"If you had taken a back kick to the nose from a rabbit with sharp claws, you would know the answer to that question as far as Walter goes."

I heard a screeching sound from the far, dark corner of the garage.

"It's a pygmy owl with a broken wing," Trevor told me. "Davie and his dad brought it over. They were walking back to their truck—they got it fixed by the way—from fishing just before dark and they found it on the path. Someone had shot it with a BB gun."

"That's not right."

"The BB was lodged in his shoulder. I removed it, used a

disinfectant, and bound the wing to his body. I'll give him a few days, then take him back to the river."

"He looks … I don't know."

"My mother said he looks like he has been drinking."

"Trevor, do you think he understands that you're helping him?"

"Well, he didn't try to peck me. I think all animals are smarter than we give them credit for. I want to live long enough to communicate with dolphins."

"They will probably have some criticism for the way we treat their oceans."

"Come into the house. I want to show you something."

As we came to the back door, Trevor told me his mother was doing yoga, her latest fad, in the living room and we needed to be quiet. We slipped into the kitchen and closed the door.

"Do you want to share a coke?" Trevor asked.

"Why not?"

"Check this out. It's a topographical map of the area just west of our shack."

"Now that baseball season is over, we should think about the three of us spending the night there."

"Oh, yeah, the big game. Did you win? That's not a 'happy we won' face."

"We won. I didn't help the team much."

"Team sports are overrated. All that depending on each other."

"What about when you are on the team to find a cure for cancer or whatever?"

"That would be different because we would all be stars."

Then I told Trevor about Mrs. Monahan being hauled away but I didn't tell him about my mother clapping. It would have been disloyal somehow. Trevor wasn't really listening.

"You're right, we should spend a night there. On a clear night. I'll bring my telescope. Look at this. The lines show any change in elevation. The closer the lines are together—"

"The steeper the hill?"

"Or the more precipitous the canyon walls."

"What canyon?"

"The canyon of no return."

"Seriously?"

"See these lines here, how close together they are? And these small numbers? I think I've found a canyon eighty feet deep that we have never been to."

"Are the beaver ponds by our shack the headwaters of a creek that runs through that canyon?"

"Maybe, there might some springs."

"It must be time to mount an expedition. An African, big game, unknown canyon type of expedition," I said.

"With Davie. All men good and true. What about concrete?"

"Just one more job next week."

"Tomorrow then? My mother promised to pack a great lunch for all of us. Don't worry, no tofu this time."

Chapter Twelve
Secret Waterfall

The next morning while the three of us were eating breakfast, a big, brand-new-looking pick-up pulled up in front of the house. The driver sounded the horn. Norton was sitting in the passenger seat. I went outside.

"Hey, Jack, we came over to say good-bye. This is my dad." He reached across Norton and we shook hands.

"Nice to meet you, Jack."

"Nice to meet you, sir," I answered.

"We're moving back to Anaheim tomorrow. Together again," said Norton.

"That's great. I mean being together again."

"We need to get going. Things to do," said Norton's dad.

"Right. Good luck with your pitching, Norton."

"Good luck with your batting, Jack."

"Thanks." They pulled away. Maybe we weren't meant to be good friends but still his leaving added to my feeling that things were changing. And school was starting in a month. I rode my bike around the block to Trevor's house. His backpack was loaded down with three lunches, water, binoculars, sketch book, and a flower identification book. We swung by the trailer park and picked up Davie. His father was outside a small sheet metal building that he used as a shop. He was working on an old motorcycle.

"Hey, Jack, Trevor. I finally found the parts I needed to get this thing running again."

"How old is it?" I asked.

"Let's see … thirty-two years. Still has some miles in her. You boys have a good time. Don't start any forest fires."

"We'll be careful, sir." Trevor answered for the three of us.

We rode our bikes to our shack and chained them together

just in case a thief came by. Trevor looked at his map and looked at the beaver ponds and the marshy terrain and decided we should climb to the top of the cliff and follow the ridge line. "In a straight line, I figure it's about two miles to the canyon."

"I'll believe it when I see it," Davie said.

I followed Trevor and Davie on our ascent. Our shack was on the last flat space. I would not want to slip and slide. We reached the top safely and walked west. After about a mile, we came to a long-abandoned logging road that seemed to go in the direction of our canyon. The road ended at a small creek.

"Look," said Trevor. "You can see by the banks that it is running as high in summer as during the winter. He scooped up some water. "Cold. Must be spring fed. We'll look for the source on the way back. I'm afraid to drink it. It might have Giardia, a water-borne parasite that makes you really sick. My dad says you used to be able to drink from streams anywhere in these mountains."

"Coffee break," said Davie, pulling a battered thermos out of his pack. We passed it around.

"It's kind of brushy but let's follow the stream," Trevor decided.

"You mean you didn't bring a weed whacker with you?" I said, teasing him.

"I'll go first," Trevor responded.

"Rattlesnakes! Here comes Trevor," Davie called out.

After a half hour, Trevor stopped. "Quiet ... I think I hear a waterfall—and the tops of those trees? They're pines instead of dwarf oaks." We listened. I imagined a small, hidden paradise. We were not disappointed. A few minutes later, we stood next to a waterfall about twenty feet high that fell into a crystal-clear pool surrounded by greenery. A "microclimate" Trevor called it. There was even a rock to dive off. We followed a deer trail down to the pool.

"I'll check to make sure the water is deep enough to dive," said Davie as he stripped down, ran across the narrow beach into the water and swam down to the bottom next to the big rock.

When he emerged, I called out, "How's the water?"

"Perfect. Eight feet deep. First dibs on diving," he said as he came out of the pool.

Perfect! He looked cold! We stripped down and followed him as he climbed up to the diving rock.

"Remember," said Trevor, "rattlesnake-wise, never put your hand or foot somewhere you can't see."

We stood on the rock. Davie launched off the rock in a perfect swan dive. It made me wish I had brought a camera. I went next with a cannonball. The water was far colder than I guessed but when I surfaced, I pretended it wasn't in order to fool Trevor who after landing somewhat flat came up sputtering and using words he would never dare use at home.

I think my friends felt it too ... as we treaded water and looked around at our little bit of paradise. *What could be better than an adventure in the woods with my two best friends?*

"To be a member of this group," Davie said, looking at Trevor, "we need to all do a back flip."

"I have a knife," Trevor said. "Can't we just slit our palms and swear a blood oath?"

"No," Davie said. "I'll coach you. It's just a matter of science."

"Really?" questioned Trevor.

We climbed back up to the rock. The warm sun felt good. Davie stood on the edge of the rock, his back to the water.

"It's all about force and gravity. By bending my knees, then straightening them while throwing my arms up and back I will generate lift and gravity will do the rest. Like this." His demonstration made it look easy.

"Okay, the science sounds good. I just need to make a commitment," said Trevor. He launched. It worked. His form wasn't perfect, but he splashed down safely. "Okay, that was almost fun but once was enough. Your turn, Jack."

I looked down at the water ten feet below me. I had done some back flips in our pool, but at home the water was right there.

"We're waiting," Davie called out.

"Jump, Jump," they chanted.

I pictured myself doing it, then went for it. Time seemed

to slow down. I rotated a little too far and landed partly on my back but, hey, I had done it.

Trevor climbed out, went to his backpack and took out a towel.

I said, "A towel? You were that confident there would be water here?"

"Yes. I'm going to leave you two aquanauts and look around for wildflowers."

Davie and I took turns doing the tricks we had done at my backyard pool. The water seemed colder each time. We stopped and lay in the sun to warm up. It felt wonderful. Partly asleep, I said, "If we were adults, we could walk from here to Canada on the Pacific Crest Trail, stopping to swim in mountain lakes."

"If we were adults, we could both buy motorcycles and ride to Alaska."

"And climb Denali?"

"Why not. Dream big."

Trevor returned looking excited.

"You'll never believe what I found!"

"I'm not going to guess," we said together. Trevor's enthusiasms were not always our enthusiasms.

"A cactus."

"Not one of those ones that are ten feet tall?" asked Davie.

"No. But have you ever seen a cactus anywhere around here?"

"No. And my dad and I go cactus hunting at least twice a month," said Davie.

"If it's a new species, I was going to name it after us, combine our names or something, but not now. I made a sketch. I'll take it to the botanist at the community college and see what he thinks."

"We're happy for you but, more importantly, is it lunch time? I'm starved," said Davie, getting back into his clothes.

Sandwiches, chips, orange juice, and fruit. "Thanks, Trevor's mom," I said.

We sat on the narrow beach. We were quiet. Each of us taking in what a beautiful place we had found. *Did people stumble across it during hunting season?* We hadn't seen any sign of man. No trash. Cumulus clouds sailed by throwing light and shadows on the landscape. I was looking at the waterfall when out of the corner of my eye, I saw a mountain lion! On top of the canyon wall. Looking straight at me. I tried to be a rock. The phrase "you're not in the wilderness until you are part of the food chain," passed through my mind. A cloud shadow swept across the canyon rim. The big cat vanished.

I looked at Davie and Trevor. They seemed lost in their own thoughts. I watched the place where the mountain lion had appeared.

"Nap time," Davie said, lying back and pulling his ball cap over his eyes. I considered not saying anything about seeing a real lion. Trevor, who is very good at reading people, said, "What is it, Jack?"

"Both of you, you know I wouldn't lie to you, make something up, unless it was part of our fantasy firefighting or whatever."

"Yah, yah, what is it? You saw a UFO circling Mt. Shasta?" teased Davie, from under his hat.

"No. Better than that. For just a few seconds, while you two were daydreaming, I saw a mountain lion on the top of the cliff."

"Did he look surprised to see us?" said Davie.

"Yes. No. I'm positive I saw him."

Trevor took a plastic bag out of his pack and held it up. "I believe you. I found this. Mountain lion scat, or poop to you."

"Are you sure?" asked Davie, sitting up.

"Yes. I just happen to have this book with me." He rummaged in his pack and took out: *A Tracker's Guide to Northern California.*

We stood up and looked around.

Trevor said, "It's a good place for a cat. Water, plenty of deer, and three miles from the nearest road. We can't tell anyone. My mom would never let me come here again."

"Why do I feel like a trespasser?" I said mostly to myself.

"This isn't the first time I've felt someone was watching

us," said Davie. "Trevor, have you seen any poop around our shack?"

"No, but I haven't been looking."

"You're not in the wilderness until you are part of the food chain," I said, out loud this time.

"Gee, Jack, thanks for sharing that bit of wisdom you read in some book."

"Don't worry, Davie. Statistically mountain lion attacks are very rare," Trevor pointed out.

"But does this particular lion know that?" Davie asked, half laughing.

Trevor took out his binoculars and scanned the cliff. "I read that they see us far more often than we see them. They're cats. They're curious. He or she could be watching us right now."

It was great seeing the mountain lion, but I felt angry. It took me a minute to figure out why. Just a few minutes ago, this bit of paradise had "belonged" to us and now it "belonged" to the lion. I knew I should be happy that with towns and highways, this mountain lion had found a home.

* * *

When I am reading an adventure story, I like to pretend I am the hero. My parents have even accused me of talking like one of the characters. Only a week before seeing a real lion, during an evening meeting at our shack—there was some grumbling that summer was getting boring—I had suggested we go on a fantasy lion hunting expedition. I had just finished reading the big game hunting stories by Earnest Hemingway and others. Sitting on the old car seat on the front porch of our shack I imagined that, instead of beaver ponds, I was looking at an African savannah. I'd decided right then that I would go to Africa someday. To act out the story, we would need someone to play the wounded lion, "the Great White Hunter," and the coward. Trevor and Davie were not enthusiastic.

"We need tall grass for the lion to hide in," objected Trevor. "Really tall grass. I'm not playing the coward. I like stories where we all get to be heroes."

"I'll play the coward," I said.

"Wait," said Davie. "I need to understand something. The wounded lion knows we're coming—right?"

"Yes. The lion is too weak to run far."

"She knows she will die?" asked Davie.

"Look, the story isn't told from the lion's point of view," I said. "Instead of tall grass, we can use the really brushy area south of the beaver dam."

"It won't be the same," complained Davie.

"It's after eight. It's shady. It will work," I said. "The lion dies a noble death," I pointed out.

"I don't want to be the Great White Hunter. Doesn't make sense for someone who might be a veterinarian someday," objected Trevor.

"Well, Jack," Davie said, "We're best friends but this story is going to be just in your head. End of an era. It was fun. Remember the time we were a commando unit? We scaled a cliff to take out an enemy machine gun nest while pretending firecrackers were grenades!"

"And almost burned the woods down!" exclaimed Trevor. "I liked the plane crash one. Middle of winter. How to survive."

"My turn," I said. "Bows and arrows. Trying to sneak up on the crows, pretending they were buffalo and we were Indians."

"Not my favorite," said Davie. "Trying to believe the crows were buffalo just didn't work."

"Imagination, Davie, imagination. We needed something hard to sneak up on. Crows were perfect."

"Whatever, you say, fearless leader," said Trevor.

"What? We should have snuck up on a herd of cows?"

"My all-time favorite was fighting the forest fire, and second place would be jousting on the log over the swamp with brooms, knocking each other into the muck," said Davie.

"Because you won every time," I said. "The dumbest one I did all by myself. Pretending to be Tarzan, jumping out of a tree, and grabbing a rope only to find out I wasn't strong enough to hold on, too high to let go, extreme rope burns on both hands!"

"Ouch!" said Davie. "Just think of the real adventures waiting for us. The day I turn eighteen and don't need my dad's permission, I'm going sky diving."

"If I want adventure this winter, all I have to do is point my skis straight down hill and let 'em rip!"

"I don't know, Jack, with all those romance novels you read, I see you falling in love."

"Adventure stories!"

"Would winning a scholarship to a national science fair count?" Trevor asked.

"Only because you're our friend," Davie answered.

Fist bumps all around.

Friends forever, we mounted our bikes and left the gloomy "African" bush, and rode into the quiet, shaded streets of our hometown with Mt. Shasta in the background, tinted light orange by the setting sun.

Chapter Thirteen
Baseball at the State Prison

I thought baseball season was over, but I had forgotten about Coach's end of the season barbecue. While we were having an apple pie and ice cream dessert, "I scream, you scream, we all scream for ice cream", Mayor Small showed up and made an announcement he thought would be applauded. He was wrong. He announced that as winners of our league, we were going to play a team from Southern Oregon at—he paused for effect—a state prison!

The words "state prison" hung in the air like barbecue smoke. A dozen young ball players stared at him thinking it must be a joke. Coach looked uneasy. (I learned later from Mom that the mayor had promised Coach some new equipment if he went along.) The mayor, well known for his pet projects, waited for applause. It didn't happen. All the parents started talking at once. When things quieted down, Mayor Small came to his own defense saying every player from Mt. Shasta would receive a certificate signed by the governor.

"We have to go. The Oregon team is already bragging they will beat us. It would be embarrassing to forfeit. If any of the fine young men on our team have the slightest chance of going wrong, then a tour of the prison should set them straight. It will be educational."

To my surprise, I saw my mother nodding her head. I didn't take it personally. She was always supporting some cause or another. My father would see her putting a check in the mail and he would get a pained look on his face. I muttered something about it being too bad Norton wasn't still in town. My mom pretended not to hear me.

"Jails are part of our society and always will be," she said. "I don't see why our kids shouldn't know what they are really like."

The general muttering continued. I decided I liked the idea. It would be an adventure to tell Davie and Trevor about. The players as a group decided playing in a prison would be "fun." Something to brag about.

* * *

The old gray prison was worse than I imagined, the inmates, even the normal looking ones, were scary. The old saying "the road to hell is paved with good intentions " went through my mind. There was a smell ... I can't describe it. And noise. I want to forget them both. Finally, we were back outside in bright sunlight. The enclosed prison courtyard was about the size of a little league field.

Our guide told us the inmates had raked the entire dirt field, built a pitcher's mound, and put out the bases. The ones on good behavior would watch from the sidelines. We greeted the members of the other team. The Star-spangled Banner, distorted, blasted out of two big speakers mounted on the walls. The words "land of the free, home of the brave" didn't ring true. Play ball!

By some unspoken agreement, pitchers on both teams threw slower speed strikes. Players often hit the first pitch. A batter for the Oregon team hit a high fly ball that carried to the catwalk overlooking center field for a home run. The inmates, for reasons of their own, went crazy with yelling. This led to the base runner grandstanding by jumping high in the air at each base and coming down with both feet on the bag. This caused more cheering.

From my viewpoint in center field, I saw the prison yard and a game of baseball being played but I didn't quite believe it. On my second turn at bat, I hit the only home run of my life so far. I did a cartwheel between third and home. The crowd went wild. The guards along the sidelines looked nervous. Home run followed home run. At the end of four innings, the score was tied twelve to twelve. Every home-run-hitting base runner tried to outdo the antics of the others.

The two coaches called an emergency meeting and declared the game tied and over with. The players refused to go back inside the prison to a conference room they had used as locker room to change clothes. The coaches and chaperones went in, gathered up our clothes to be sorted out by the main gate where we waited as if we were being released from a ten-year sentence.

On the bus ride home, we mostly pretended to be napping. No one talked about the experience. I guessed the mayor would lose his next election.

Chapter Fourteen
After Dinner Entertainment

I was sitting on our back porch with my parents when Trevor stuck his head over the top of our back fence. "Are you ready for some after dinner entertainment?" he called out.

My mom answered, "With you Trevor, I'm not sure what the right answer is."

"Well, Mrs. Iverson, you can watch over the fence. You don't have to walk around the block."

"Trevor. I could climb over that fence if I wanted to," Mom answered firmly.

We ambled over. Walter, the basset hound, was tied up to the picnic table. Oscar, the rabbit, was on a leash. Trevor had been taking him for walks. "I'm going to let Walter chase Oscar but don't worry. Even if he does catch up with the rabbit, he's afraid of being kicked. I guarantee the rabbit will win."

With that, Trevor unhooked Oscar from his leash. Walter stared at Oscar. Oscar ignored him. Trevor untied Walter. Walter went for the rabbit. Oscar ran down the backside of the garage and turned the corner and ran down the length of the garage. There is only a six-inch gap between the wall of the garage and the fence. The rabbit turned the corner nearest us and stopped. Walter appeared at the far end of the narrow passage. I could see him thinking: *No rabbit. It must be on the other side of the garage.*

Walter turned around and ran. Somehow Oscar knew this. He rounded the corner and ran back down the narrow passage and disappeared around the corner just as Walter arrived at the end nearest us. Walter went through the same thought process and ran. Oscar ran down the passageway and ducked around the corner.

"How long does this go on?" my dad asked.

"Until Walter falls down exhausted and pretends to take a nap. This way I don't have to take him for walks."

"He never catches the rabbit, and he never gives up until he just can't go on," Mom said.

Dad commented. "There is no life lesson here, Irene, except this particular rabbit is smarter than this particular dog."

"Maybe I could borrow dogs from around the neighborhood and run some experiments."

"What if you found a dog that was smarter than the rabbit? That could end badly," I said.

"Yeah, I guess."

"Thanks for the entertainment," Mom said.

We went back to our porch. "Other than getting all A's, how does that boy do in school?" Mom asked in a way that she didn't really expect an answer.

"Jack?" Dad prompted.

"The truth? He is well liked, partly because he … he often corrects teachers or makes some comment that makes kids laugh. And he can draw. He draws cartoons of teachers, not nasty ones. Some of the teachers put them on their bulletin boards."

"He doesn't get bullied then?" Mom asked.

"No. At the end of last school year, he stopped a bully by walking over and stepping between the bully and the victim. When the guy tried to push Trevor aside, he did some kind of police hold on a nerve in the bully's shoulder. Knocked him right to his knees, then Trevor just walked away. It was all over before I could help. I asked him how he had learned to do that and he just said, 'From a book. You can learn anything from a book.'"

"Speaking of which," Dad said. "The library is still open, let's drive over."

Chapter Fifteen
Time with my Own Kind

In the five days after the prison baseball game, I mowed eighteen lawns; both my regular customers and people going on vacation who needed their lawn mowed just once. Meanwhile Davie and Trevor were building the tree fort without me. The day after I caught up with my lawn jobs, I lay in bed listening to the sound of my parents' voices in the kitchen. All was well except that between the Mrs. Monahan drama, Saturday morning concrete, the baseball game in the prison, lawn mowing and my parents, I had spent too much of my life lately with adults. I decided I needed to spend time with my own kind. I needed to spend time with Trevor and Davie. So, I waited until my parents left for the day. Outside my door, I heard Mom say, "Let him sleep in if he wants."

I made my own breakfast. I mowed my one lawn, (the biggest on my list, even though it was a little early for a noisy lawnmower) came back home, packed up some lunches and pedaled off to search for the "highest tree fort built by kids ever." I locked my bike to the porch railing of our shack and headed south in what I knew to be the generally right direction. I practiced my tracking skills by looking for bent grass, bent sticks. I didn't need to. Either Trevor or Davie had tied pieces of red ribbon on tree branches to mark the way. After a while, I was able to follow the sound of hammering.

I couldn't believe it when I reached the tall ponderosa pine. At least thirty feet up was a nearly completed platform. Davie and Trevor were busy nailing down the last of the flooring.

"Hey, Jack! Nice of you to show up when the work is almost done."

"I was busy," I yelled back, tilting my head to see them.

"Yeah, yeah," said Davie. "Hitting a home run at the state prison."

"Whatever. Now that I'm here what can I do for you gentlemen?"

Trevor answered, "Make a pizza run."

I ignored him.

Davie called down. "In the bushes behind the shack is a small pile of lumber. It's for a handrail. We weren't going to have one but it's pretty scary up here."

"I believe that. So you want me to hike back—"

"Three times," said Trevor.

Davie leaned out over the edge of the platform and said, "We'll all go, one trip, then finish the railing."

"Can I come up first to check it out?"

"Sure, why not," Davie said.

I wondered why he was laughing. There was a long rope ladder from the ground to the first branch. Davie had cut the boards at home, drilled holes in them for the rope, and tied knots for each board to keep them in place. I started to climb. The ladder twisted and swung sideways, making it hard to get my foot onto the next step. I hung on until it settled. Trevor's voice came down from above. "There's a trick to it."

"Are you going to tell me what it is?" I asked through clenched teeth.

Two "no's" floated down.

I tried again. I made three steps. The twisting ladder made me stop climbing. I started up again. This time I was careful to push straight down on the next step instead of partly sidewards and I pulled on the ropes above the steps equally with both hands. It worked.

"By George, I think he's got it," Trevor said to Davie, his voice sounding nearer than it had before. In a few more minutes, I reached the end of the rope ladder and the first branch on the tree. I climbed higher. Some of the branches were close together but two were just far enough apart to be a challenge. I tried not to look down or think about falling. Finally, I reached the platform and, with Davie's help, made it through the opening in the deck and flopped down, winded and sweaty. After a minute, I got to my feet and held onto the tree.

The view sure was worth the climb! To the northeast, snowcapped Mt. Shasta was visible all the way down to tree line. It shone brilliantly white against a perfect blue sky. I could make out three church steeples showing above the trees in town. To the north was the perfect volcanic shape of Cinder Cone. Trevor handed me binoculars and pointed to a nearby snag. In the broken top of the tree was a large nest. Through the glasses, I could see a nesting bald eagle.

"Incredible, Trevor," I said. Just then a gust of wind came up and the tree swayed. I almost dropped the binoculars as I instinctively grabbed the tree.

"You get used to it," Davie said.

"Wow," I exclaimed. "How did you get this built? You're braver than I thought."

"These three branches gave me a place to start," answered Davie. "I stayed up here while Trevor cut pieces on the ground. I hauled them up with a rope. It seemed much safer once half the platform was built."

"But how did you get the rope ladder up to the first branches?" I asked.

"I climbed the tree using a pair of lineman's spikes and a harness strap. My uncle used to work for the phone company. You just put the strap around the tree, dig in the spikes, lean back and shimmy up the tree. It was fun."

"You are the only junior high guy I know who would be brave enough to do that," I said.

"Meanwhile, you are still holding on to the tree," Trevor teased.

I let go and took a short step away. "My friends, I salute you. It will be an honor to hike out for the handrail materials because I am never coming up here again without one."

"We'll go with you but first there is an initiation."

"You aren't going to tell me I have to pee over the side!?"

"Gee," said Davie, "we hadn't thought of that. No, you just have to stand at the edge and look down until you're not afraid."

"Within certain time limits," Trevor added.

"Don't worry, Jack. I'll hold on to the back of your shirt," said Davie.

I inched forward. I wasn't afraid of heights when I was on a chairlift at the ski area or on the Ferris wheel at the county fair, but this was different. My best friends ever were waiting. I inched forward. Davie stayed with me. I stood at the edge. I looked down. I kept looking down until down was just down. I stepped back. I high fived my friends.

"The things our parents don't want to know," I said, not quite knowing what I meant.

"You mean if they ask us how high the fort is we'll just say 'high enough' for a good view. I'm vague all the time with my parents about my science experiments. Besides they don't tell us everything about their lives so fair is fair."

The bald eagle rose from its nest with a heavy beating of its wings and flew by us. *Was he checking us out?*

"Yesterday, I saw him fly by with a fish so big he had to work really hard to stay airborne," said Trevor.

"There are times when I wish I was a bird so I could fly away," said Davie.

There was some emotion in his voice which surprised me. We watched the eagle ride the updrafts, then sail away toward the river.

We climbed down and shared the extra sandwiches I had made. We hauled in the boards for the handrail. I joined Davie at the platform while Trevor cut parts and sent them up.

We finished up just in time to get home for dinner. My mother had a fool proof system. If I was five minutes late, she put my meal in the refrigerator. If I was ten minutes late, she promised to put it in the freezer. It never happened. Just the thought of staring at a pork chop waiting for it to get back to room temperature was enough to get me home on time.

We were packed up and ready to go but Trevor was looking up at our tree fort. Davie and I looked at each other. We knew when Trevor got quiet, something was about to happen.

"All we need now is a steady, windy day so we can go up there and experience what is like to be a tree in the wind."

"I don't want to be a tree in the wind, I want to be a boy who survives the summer," said Davie.

Trevor said, "Don't give me that look! Have I ever steered you wrong"?

"Well," I said, "there was the time we slept in the cemetery to prove to ourselves that ghosts don't exist, stayed up half the night talking, and we were still asleep when the family members showed up to—"

"Other than that," Trevor interrupted.

"Or the time we climbed onto the roof of the new skating rink and the wind blew the ladder down and we had to yell for help for like an hour until someone called the police," I argued. "And when you almost electrocuted the dog—"

"I prefer to think of it as an attitude adjustment—"

"And I had to lie to protect you when the dog's owner asked if I knew anything about the incident."

"Well, yes, but still, we need at least one more adventure before school starts."

"It's okay, Trevor. We'll come with you," said Davie.

"All for one, one for all," I added.

Chapter Sixteen
A Good Life

Professor Ballard has the largest lawn on my list. Their house, easily the fanciest and largest in the neighborhood, is on a triple-sized lot surrounded by trees with a lap pool in the back and a small building full of work-out equipment. It's at the top of a hill. From their kitchen patio, you can see the top of Mt. Shasta.

He pays well. I am only allowed to mow between eleven and twelve on Thursday mornings. In winter, a plow takes care of the driveway and I shovel the sidewalk and the back patio. I need to be done by 6:30 a.m. Unlike people on our street with regular jobs, Professor Ballard writes books: six biographies and two travel books so far. My parents bought them all. I liked his travel book about his motorcycle journey from Alaska to Argentina.

Professor Ballard also teaches English literature at our community college. I knew he had once been a teacher at Stanford. His wife, Suzanne, explained to me that he didn't like "academic types" at the famous university. He said his students at the community college here are "real" people and he loved being a member of the mountaineering club. She told me his best friend is "Dan, the Backhoe Man." They ski and fish together and shoot billiards, she added.

Usually, Mrs. Ballard meets me on the back patio with an iced tea or, in winter, a hot chocolate, but today she invited me in to see the house for the first time.

Professor Ballard was in the kitchen. He called out, "Jack, I appreciate your reliability, thought you might like a tour of the house."

The living room has a stone fireplace bordered by two abstract stained-glass windows. The west wall is almost all glass with a view of a Japanese rock garden complete with a miniature waterfall.

"He brought up a designer and two workers from San Francisco to install it." Mrs. Ballard informed me. The other two walls are covered by books, expensive looking books, on fancy wood shelves. I never knew one person could own so many books!

"Three thousand, one hundred and nine, exactly."

"You counted them?"

"I order and check in all the books he buys for his research. I took over the record keeping from his previous wife."

"He's read them all?"

"Except for the ones pulled out an inch. I read the table of contents of each new book and write a summary, correspond with the publishers, editors, and type clean copies of his messy pages. This house is set up to help my husband in his writing. The pool is for exercise breaks, the large lot for privacy. This is the billiard room. It has a special ventilator to get rid of cigar smoke. When his cronies show up, I often go to a movie. Here's the door to his office. See the green light there? If it's lit, I can knock. Red means do not disturb unless the house is on fire! A desk. And a great stereo system, hundreds of classical records. No phone."

"All this just to write a book?"

"Not just any book. Out there in the big world, he's quite famous. Around here, I guess people see him as an eccentric who rides a bicycle, almost always wears a tie, and has a habit of marrying younger women," she said with a smile.

I didn't know what to say. That was exactly the way we did see him!

"This house is a reward for writing a bestselling book."

"The one about General Lee and the Civil War? I read it … well, some of it. My dad liked it."

"Still his biggest seller. He drew the plans for this house when he was sixteen and had it built when he was thirty. And this is my office and music room. Sound proofed with great acoustics. The violin is my passion. I play in a quartet. Did you know the violin is the closest instrument to the human voice? Let me show you something special."

Mrs. Ballard took a violin out of its case and tuned it. She showed me how to hold it and on which strings to put two of my fingers, then she stood behind me and ran the bow over the strings. The sound went through my side directly to my heart. I couldn't believe it.

"Did it, the notes, go directly to your heart?"

"Yes. That's exactly how it felt."

Professor Ballard called from the kitchen. "Lunch is ready. Don't forget to give Jack his present."

"I told him your whole family loves to read," Suzanne whispered. She walked me to the back door and handed me a book wrapped in brown paper. "It's *Alone* by Admiral Byrd. First edition, autographed."

I knew this was a big deal. "I couldn't," I said quietly.

"It's all right. He feels that every reader should own one truly great book. You wouldn't think a book about a man alone in a shack in the Antarctic would be interesting, but it is."

I left their house thinking how great it must be to … well, live your life just like you wanted to. I felt good, encouraged maybe. *What would I make of my life?* I coasted down the hill on my bike to our house. There were no cars parked on the street, so I made wide sweeping turns from curb to curb.

There was a "For Sale" sign on Mrs. Monahan's lawn! The grass was a little long and the flowers looked like they needed watering. I made myself a peanut butter and jelly sandwich, then took care of business. That night, I decided to read myself to sleep with my new book, but Mrs. Ballard had been right. It was fascinating. I read until my eyes got tired, I read until closing one eye didn't keep me going. Even though it was a warm summer night, I read wrapped in a sleeping bag.

Chapter Seventeen
Act of Courage

It was a windy day. While I was eating lunch, I saw Trevor climb over our back fence and walk toward our back door with a gleam in his eyes. I thought of hiding but if no one answered the door, he would probably just barge in. Davie and I had promised him that on the next windy day when we were all free, we would climb up to the "world's highest tree fort built by middle school students." There was no way to get out of doing it without being labeled a coward.

"Hey, Trevor, glad to see you on this windy day! I can't wait to climb the tree!" I figured if I had to pretend to be brave, I would go all out.

"Based on scientific observations before we built the fort, my estimate is we will have an arc of six feet. It should be enough for you to experience what it would be like in the crow's nest of an old sailing ship like in the books you read."

"You guarantee that it's not going to blow over?"

"Absolutely, it's a healthy tree. I called Davie. We can meet him at his trailer."

"Okay, let me finish lunch."

"You're not worried about getting seasick up there in the crow's nest?"

"Should I be?"

"No. Simply a case of mind over matter. I'll go home and leave my mom a note."

When we got to Davie's trailer, he was sitting on his father's motorcycle.

"Where are you headed motorcycle man?" I called out.

"Nowhere special," he said as he mounted his bicycle.

On the dirt road into the woods, the wind blew dirt from

our tires into the air. It seemed to be getting stronger. Davie and I dropped behind Trevor and exchanged a look.

"Is this a good idea?" Davie mouthed.

I shook my head. But we didn't turn back. The swaying trees beside the road were making a series of noises: squeaks, groans, and sometimes a sound like a baby crying. It was a little spooky. When we arrived, our tree fort looked higher off the ground than I remembered. Trevor started to climb. The rope ladder didn't seem to sway any more than usual. Trevor disappeared through the opening in the deck, then re-appeared waving to us. Even from the ground, I could tell he was happy.

Davie and I flipped a coin to see who would go next. I lost. When I made it onto the deck, Trevor was standing with legs braced far apart facing the wind and laughing. I tried to stand up and immediately fell to my knees. I crawled to the tree and hung on. I watched Trevor.

"I love this!" he shouted into the wind.

Davie's head appeared in the opening. He didn't look happy. This turned out to be the only time in our long friendship that Trevor turned out to be braver than Davie.

"I feel dizzy. Help me!"

I crawled back to the opening and taking hold of his upper arms, helped him onto the platform. We lay there watching Trevor. He seemed to have forgotten about us. I watched how he shifted his weight and flexed his knees in tune with the swaying tree. I decided I could either copy him or crawl to the edge of the platform and throw up. I got to my feet, my arms spread wide for balance. Davie joined me. We faced into the wind. We rode the wind. I felt a wonderful equilibrium. We all looked at each other and laughed. It felt great! I loved the feel of wind on my face, my body standing strongly with the wind. I watched the swaying of the treetops. I slowly turned and faced Mt. Shasta rising above the storm clouds. It had never looked more beautiful. From its snow-covered summit plumes of windblown snow trailed to the east.

I felt like I was flying. I was unafraid. I knew that this adventure was something we would all remember for the rest of our lives.

Chapter Eighteen
Allison Arrives

The next day when I got back from mowing three lawns there was a "Sold" sign on the front lawn of Mrs. Monahan's house. I would need to send her nephew a final bill for taking care of the lawn. Inside, my mother had left a note telling me to clean my room. While I was doing that, I heard the dinging of a truck backing into Mrs. Monahan's driveway. I went to my bedroom window. A girl about my age was directing a backing rental truck.

She had long brown hair, was wearing shorts and an Elvis Presley t-shirt. She saw me standing in the window, she didn't smile. It must have looked like I was spying on her. I stepped back and I wondered if I should help them unload. I heard the sliding back door of the truck bang open, heard the ramp being pulled out. I decided to introduce myself. Why not? The girl already knew I was home. I went into the bathroom and looked at myself in the mirror. I don't know why. When I went outside, the new people were on their front porch trying to open the door. The girl kicked the door.

"Hi, I'm Jack Iverson, next door. Trouble?"

"I'm Jim Schultz and this is my daughter, Allison."

Allison didn't say anything. She looked "perturbed," a word I had discovered recently which seemed to fit a lot of situations. "The real estate people seem to have given me the wrong key."

"I've been mowing the lawn. Her nephew gave me a key. I'll be right back."

When I returned with the key, Mr. Schultz shook my hand and thanked me. "Can you add our lawn to your list? I'm not really into yard work."

I glanced at Allison.

"Don't look at me," she said. "I have better things to do."

"Allison isn't happy about moving here from Michigan."

"Don't talk for me please," she responded. "Here looks okay but I miss my friends."

"I'd be happy to help you unload," I said.

"You're hired. If the three of us work," he said, "then Allison and I can go for a motorcycle ride, check out the town."

"Oh, okay," Allison said, brightening up a bit.

Jim is a man of medium height, slender, athletic looking, but I noticed when we shook hands, his hand felt soft, unlike my dad's work hardened ones. He looked a little pale, as if he hadn't spent much time outdoors lately. On the other hand, Allison looked like she had spent the entire summer outside. Her nose was peeling, and her legs and arms were dark brown. Her left knee was scabbed and there were fresh scratches on her arms.

We didn't talk much while we worked. Among the few household items ("We're going to buy all new furniture," Mr. Schultz told me) were two bikes, tennis equipment, skateboards, a two-person kayak, and two pairs of skis.

I admit it. While we worked, I kept glancing at Allison. Was she eying me? The last thing to unload was a large, custom painted motorcycle. Its red paint and chrome shone bright even in the shadows of the moving van. There were flames painted on the gas tank. I thought it was a work of art.

"I get to ride it when I turn eighteen," Allison said.

Mr. Schultz undid the safety straps, wheeled the bike back and forth until it was facing the back of the truck and lined up with the ramp. "I rode it up the ramp," he said, "I guess I can ride it down." The front wheel bounced when it came off the ramp but Mr. Schultz held on and brought it safely to a halt. "Add a reasonable amount for helping us unload to your lawn mowing bill, Jack. Let's take a look at the backyard. I flew in and out for an interview with the college and only briefly visited the house before I bought it."

"I mow it once a week, water the flowers once a week, the lawn twice a week, and do a little weeding."

"Besides the mowing, that all sounds like something Allison can do to earn her keep."

"It's a deal," I answered but I wondered if Allison would be thrilled. Just then she came out of the house carrying two helmets and two leather jackets.

"Okay. A short ride then we need to return the rental truck."

I watched them ride away. Did Allison give me a little half wave? I wasn't sure. And why had I hung around as they were getting ready to leave instead of going home? I got on my bike and pedaled over to the dry cleaners to tell my mother about our new neighbors.

"Is she cute, our new neighbor?" Mom asked.

"I guess," I answered blushing. I hate it when I blush. "She didn't act all that friendly."

"Give her some time. We moved three times between junior high and high school when I was growing up. It's hard. Maybe we can invite them over for a cookout in a week or so."

"Allison skateboards. Maybe we can go to the skate park."

"What happens if she is better than you?"

"I'll take it like a man," I said laughing.

"They are sure to be an improvement over Mrs. Monahan. I still feel bad about celebrating when she left. What about the Mom?"

"They didn't say."

"The neighborhood grape vine will let us know."

"Sometimes I wish I lived in a town where people minded their own business. I did find out that he's a retired fireman. He's the new head of the Fire Technology department at the college."

"Please take some steaks out of the freezer when you get home. What are you doing with the rest of your day?"

"One lawn to mow. Reading Slocum's book about sailing around the world alone. There's supposed to be a tag football game happening at the park. Davie and I might check it out. He has a shot at starting halfback but I've decided not to play. I want to add some customers to my list to earn enough for a season pass at the mountain."

"Does your father know about this? He'll be disappointed."

"Not yet. I guess he'll be disappointed but really, I'm not

fast enough to play a safety or big enough to be a lineman. I'll tell him tonight."

"I can do it for you if you want."

"No, thanks. Can you help me write and print a flier? I want to add a few snow shoveling jobs even if I have to get up really early to finish before school."

"You know I wanted to ski with you more last year but adult passes are expensive."

"That's okay. They're running a free shuttle bus this year. So I can go on my own, right?"

"Yes."

I was already thinking about skiing with Allison. Was I crazy? Summer wasn't even over and I was making imaginary ski dates with Allison, who hadn't even talked to me yet. *Get a grip.*

My skiing had possibilities. I loved being out in the cold, clear mountain air, even on secondhand skis and wearing ski clothes from the local thrift store. I went skiing just three times last year with my mother who I would describe as a graceful but cautious skier. I did my best to copy her. But when she quit before the lifts closed and I took a few runs on my own, I would ski as I dared, not caring if I looked graceful or not.

All summer long, I read adventure books and all summer long, I looked at Mt. Shasta and thought my future would have something to do with mountains.

Over the next few days, Allison and her dad came and went on his motorcycle and delivery trucks with furniture and carpets and appliances showed up. A used, beat-up Chevy station wagon appeared in the driveway. After two days of not having an excuse to talk to her, I decided to be a hero by knocking on her door after supper and asking her if she wanted to go to the skateboard park with me.

"I saw it. It's not much, but okay."

On the way over, I wondered if I had made a mistake. Her riding technique was strong. I had trouble keeping up with her.

"I met your friend, Trevor. He's very smart, isn't he?"

"Yes. Did he invite you to his garage—to see his experiments?"

When Allison answered "No," I felt a sense of relief. *Did I have a rival already?*

"It was mostly my father and his mother who talked at the grocery store. He'll be taking a science class at the high school, and I'll be taking a math class there."

"That's great. Welcome to the town's one and only skateboard park."

"The features are all … low. We might have to come up with creative ways to have fun. I'll race you around the perimeter three times."

Without waiting for me to answer, she took off, pumping, then curving around the first corner. I caught up with her on the next straight away. At the next corner, we almost crashed. I pulled back and she stayed in front the rest of the race, finishing just ahead of me. I was glad we were the only ones at the park. After a half hour of just barely matching Allison's maneuvers, we decided to head home.

Halfway there, Allison announced, "I have an idea. Why don't we do a fund raising to pay for better features at the park? I mean, why just accept things the way they are."

I was doubtful but when she said, "We could work together on it," I was more interested.

Chapter Nineteen
Friends

Ten days before the start of school, late in the morning, Allison and I rode over to the skateboard park on our bikes. She brought a tape measure and a clipboard. We spent some time measuring the park and making sketches of how the features could be improved. We planned to present our plans to the town's Parks and Recreation Department. On the way home, we stopped at the Frosty Freeze for milk shakes. We sat on a picnic table, our feet on the seat. We were quiet. I guessed that Allison had something on her mind.

"I didn't have that many friends where I lived before, that is, before my mother died ... a few friends stayed by me, others, I don't know, didn't want to deal with death, I guess. They drifted off, then we decided to move here. My mom and I, we were such good friends! My dad tries to make up for—maybe I should give him more of a chance. You talk to your parents?"

"Yes. Sometimes. I mean, we get along."

"If we are going to be friends, I think I should tell you about my mom."

"Okay."

"My father forgot to get gas. I heard him say he would get gas on the way home. My mother forgot to check. Damn. That's all there was to it. She had a meeting in another town to help start a children's reading program. The car ran out of gas on the way there, in the dark, on a curve on a narrow road without a shoulder. A truck came around the corner just as she was getting out of the car. It knocked our car over the bank and ran her down ..."

"That's terrible."

"It is terrible. Nothing to be done about it. Don't worry, I'm not going to cry."

"I'm not worried. I just don't know what to say."

"Maybe I shouldn't have said anything. We're not really friends, yet."

"I'd like to be," I said as she leaned against me. I gave her a quick "we're not really friends yet" side hug.

"Enough of this," Allison said. "I'll race you home."

We mounted our bikes but she didn't take off. "I think if my brain worked better, it just doesn't work as well as I want it to—do you know that feeling? If I was better at understanding people, better at forgiveness maybe, then I would be happier. My mother was very good at understanding people. Sometimes I try so hard to figure something out my head hurts."

"Like Mrs. Monahan?" I asked. I had told her the whole story including the neighbor's standing ovation when she was sent away.

"Yes. I didn't tell you. On the back of a closet shelf, I found a photo album. It looks like from her honeymoon in Yosemite National Park. She and her husband look happy so how did she get to be so unhappy in the end? Anyway, I need to talk about my dad. I think I'm pushing him away because I somehow blame him for my mother's death. Not somehow. I do blame him. He knows this but we don't talk about it."

"That sounds hard."

"We can only be friends if you never repeat anything special I tell you—promise?"

"Yes. Cross my heart and hope to die." Then I said something stupid: "Can I kiss you?"

"Not now. When I'm happier."

"All right."

We rode home together without racing. When we got home, Mom was unloading a week's supply of groceries. We helped her carry them into the house.

"Did you have a good time?" she asked.

Allison bit her lip but didn't answer.

"We made sketches of how the skateboard park should be if we can talk the city into making improvements," I answered.

"Some old people think every other teenager is a delinquent. Talk about keeping kids out of trouble. That will help."

"Trevor and his parents are on a road trip to San Diego," Jack said. "They offered to stop at a few towns and take photos of their skateboard parks and maybe get positive comments from people on the city councils."

"That's kind of them. Why don't you two wash up and I'll make us some lunch. You can show Allison the swimming pool."

"It's homemade but it gets a lot of use. My friends and I run up the ramp, do tricks. My dad, he's trying to quit smoking, uses it for exercise. My mom, on some Fridays, invites her three best friends over for a 'country club' pool party."

"It's great. I wonder if your mom and I could be friends?"

"Sure, why not. Let's go in and see if lunch is ready."

"I heard about your mom, Allison, not the details, but you know how people talk. I'm so sorry. I can't imagine."

"It was tough. I couldn't face going to school, so I home schooled with my aunt. It only took us two hours a day to cover the required material."

"So, you're completely caught up?" Mom asked with some concern.

"More than that, in math anyway. I'm going to be taking math classes at the high school this year."

"What did you do the rest of the day? After putting in your two hours?" I asked.

"We did the housework while dancing to really loud music."

"What a good idea, Jack. Perhaps you and I could dance and dust?"

"I don't think so," I said as Mom and Allison laughed.

"I already clean my room and do my own laundry," I said in self-defense.

"My aunt's Italian. She taught me to cook. After she taught me to shop. A good meal starts with shopping. I'm glad you have a decent grocery store here. And every afternoon, we would play racquetball. It helped me work of some off the anger I felt over the accident. I love the way you can really smash the ball. Therapeutic violence."

There was a pause as Mom dished up BLT's, chips, and a salad.

"Trevor, our neighborhood genius, taught himself to cook. He says it's like doing a chemistry experiment," I said.

"I don't know about that. You have to put in some love when you cook," said Allison.

"I always seem to be in a rush," Mom said.

"Maybe we could cook a meal together while the men watch football or something?"

"We don't have a TV," my mother said with some pride.

"We hardly watch it. Who has the time? Especially after school starts. Just because my dad is smart, he expects me to get all A's."

"We allow Jack a few B's. But really, going to school is your job."

"That and taking care of my dad. I guess I never paid attention to how much work my mother did."

"Jack. Are you paying attention?"

"No," I said, laughing. "I want to talk about something else besides housework. Skiing! I saw skis when I helped you unload," I said.

"One pair belonged to my mom. I can't make myself give them away. A few more years and I will be big enough to use them ..."

"I am so sorry about your mother," Mom said again. I felt both of them were close to tears. I wondered if I should make an excuse and leave the room. Silence.

"The mountains in Michigan are just hills really. Mt. Shasta is incredible," Allison said to break the silence. "I know the lifts don't go to the top but still it's a big ski area."

"Maybe," Mom said, "we could all, I mean us, William, your dad, could drive up to the ski area, hike to the top of the lift, great view of Mt. Shasta, get a feeling for the ski terrain. I don't think you will be disappointed. This weekend maybe?"

"Sounds great. I'll check with James—my dad. I'm calling him James now that we're doing the shopping together and

I'm doing the cooking. I don't know, it just seems that we are, like, partners."

"Allison. If you ever feel the need for a little woman to woman talk, I live right next door."

I must have looked worried because Mom added, "Don't worry, Jack, I promise not to talk about you as long as you promise to talk to each other."

"We do talk. Honest."

"Starting today," Allison said with a quick look at me.

The hike sounded great, but I was worried that my dad, with his bad lungs might not be able to keep up. Just then there was a honk from a car on the street. Allison jumped up and looked out the window.

"Our new car!" she said and ran outside.

By the time I got to the front porch she was getting into a blue Chevy sedan. She waved as her father pulled away from the curb.

For the next two weeks, Allison always seemed to be on her way somewhere. The planned hike to the ski area didn't happen. She did join my mother and her friends for a last of the season "pool party." I kind of wondered what Allison looked like in a bathing suit. I knew what I looked like in a bathing suit! It was obvious to me that my seventh-grade health teacher was right about girls maturing faster than boys and sometimes being more athletic.

Chapter Twenty
Rain and a Kiss in the Library

Three days to the beginning of school! When I woke up, it was raining so I rolled over and went back to sleep. In my sleep, I heard a rat-a-tatting on a drum. It was a very annoying sound. Wait! I was awake and someone was drumming their fingertips on my windowpane. I came fully awake with one thought—Allison! I pulled up the shade just as I realized I was in my underwear—too late. It was Allison. She didn't seem to notice. She was dressed in a yellow rain jacket topped by a huge Maine lobsterman rain hat. She pushed her face close to the glass.

"I'm going to the library. Do you want to walk with me?"

Still groggy from sleep, I stupidly asked why.

"To get a book dummy. Do you want to come or not?"

"Yes, absolutely. Give me a couple of minutes."

"No one answered the door. Your parents must be at work. I'll wait on the front porch."

I had never gotten dressed so fast in my life. We walked down the street to a small park then followed a narrow path next to the railroad tracks. I stepped back and let Allison go first. Part of the way, she walked balanced on the slick rail, placing one foot carefully in front of the other. I tried to copy her, but I kept slipping off. She didn't look back. She didn't even look back when she called out through the rain, "I like you, Jack Iverson."

I called back. "I like you, Allison Schultz."

"What a name I have. Maybe I'll have to marry you some day. Allison Iverson has a nicer sound to it."

"I might just do that," I said but perhaps not loud enough for her to hear.

When we turned away from the tracks a few blocks from the library, Allison reached out her hand and I took it. Happy in the rain. We walked to the library, not talking but looking at each other and smiling.

We took off our coats in the foyer. We were alone. We stood close to each other. There was something warm and comfortable about being in the library on a rainy day. Kissing seemed silly in a way but at the same time, right then, it seemed more important to me than all the wisdom in all the books in the library.

"That's enough, Jack."

"Was it okay?"

"Yes, yes, yes."

I still had my arms around her when I heard the front door open and felt a draft. It was Mr. Hawkins. He was to be our English teacher. He had a reputation for being demanding and strict. We broke apart.

"Since this is a library, I suggest you continue your journey into romance by taking a look at the love sonnets of Shakespeare."

Allison laughed and asked if he was a teacher.

"Arthur Hawkins, Esquire, at least until school starts, then I become the feared MR. HAWKINS!"

Giving him a big smile, she replied, "Allison Schultz, your future student."

I couldn't believe it! Allison was charming the socks off him.

"I shall expect nothing but excellence from you, Miss Schultz," said Mr. Hawkins as he turned to hang up his coat. Following his suggestion, we took a volume of Shakespeare's sonnets to a quiet corner of the reading room and tried reading them out loud. We decided that there was way too much unhappiness in adult love. Before checking out three books each, not sharing the titles with each other, we sat by the fire and looked at a magazine article on climbing Mount Everest.

"Maybe I'll be the first woman to climb Everest," Allison whispered, looking directly into my eyes.

"Why not?" I said.

We walked home under wind-torn clouds with the sun sometimes showing through. A train came by while we were on the narrow path next to the tracks. The sound and the wind almost knocked us over. We screamed until it felt like our brains would fall out. We screamed knowing no one could possibly hear us. It was something all the kids did if caught by a train.

When we got home, we sat on my front porch and talked. About books. About life in a small town. Skateboarding. Everything except what was on my mind.

"Are we going steady?" I finally asked.

"I don't want to call us anything. I don't want to make a big deal of ... us. No clinging. I don't go in for all that talking with other girls about boys, wasting time on the phone. We don't have to keep it secret, just, you know."

Chapter Twenty-One
Dad Gets Busted

It was my eighth and last year in the old brick schoolhouse. The building seemed to squat in the middle of its scruffy lawn like a giant toad. Summer had not been boring. I wanted to yell out, "I don't deserve to be locked up in this building for nine months." I knew what it would smell like on the first day: floor wax, new clothes, dust, and some of the girls would be wearing perfume.

"Jack! Are you all right? The building won't eat you."

I knew the voice. Ariel. I knew I was in trouble. Ariel and I had almost started dating the last week of school or our friends had said we should or something. I had forgotten all about her over the summer. I looked around. The bell hadn't rung. There was no escape.

"Great news. My mom is friends with the school secretary. She assigned us side by side lockers."

"Did you have a good summer?" I asked as I scanned the sidewalk for Allison.

"I learned to surf. You don't seem happy to see me?"

"It's not that, it's just that ..."

Allison's dad pulled up across the street and she got out of the car.

"Who's that? You're staring at her!"

"Well, maybe it would be a good idea if you changed lockers."

"Really? Fine. You are such a loser," she said as she stomped off.

Allison watched Ariel disappear into the building. "An old girlfriend of yours?"

"I am an innocent man. Our friends tried to push us together."

"So there might be some confusion about who's your girl?" Allison asked in a serious tone, but her eyes were smiling.

"I'm not confused."

"Nor am I. She doesn't stand a chance."

We walked into the building without holding hands but, somehow, I think everyone knew we were together.

* * *

Last period of the day: algebra. The only subject I really didn't like. Allison was at the high school for advanced math. I know it made sense to her but not to me. Hot. No air conditioning. I stayed awake because for the last twenty minutes we had to take a math skills test with some algebra questions.

Davie was really good at it. "It is like putting a motorcycle back together like my dad did last summer. You just figure where the parts go and put them there. I like the fact there is only one right answer."

Trevor decided he didn't like algebra because "It's like an experiment that's already been done a thousand times and someone already knows the answer."

"Are you going to get a B?" I teased him. "What would your parents do?"

"I don't know but it might be an interesting experiment."

"You don't need to worry, Jack," teased Davie. "I bet a certain young lady would be glad to tutor you well into the night."

"Careful," I said. Davie looked at me funny.

When we were released from "prison," I was surprised to see my dad's truck parked across the street. This was so unusual I was afraid something had happened to my mother.

"What's wrong?" I shouted as I opened the passenger door and jumped in. "Is Mom okay?"

"It's nothing like that. I just wanted to talk to you. I have good news and not so good news."

"Good news first."

"I've just been to the doctor and my lungs are doing better. Three months now since I smoked. They will never fully recover but, still, an improvement."

"That's great. And the bad news?"

"I've been cited for working without a license or permit. The carport. I mean what's the big deal? There's no electric or plumbing. Just some posts and a roof."

"You don't have to tear it down, do you?"

"No. A two hundred dollar fine and I'm blocked from getting a contractor's license for six months."

"So much for being self-employed."

"That's okay. My boss has projects lined up through the winter."

"You weren't, like, arrested?"

"No! It's a civil case, not criminal. My name won't be in the paper."

"That's good. I can't tell if you really did anything wrong."

"Well, I broke the rules. I knew what they were. Lots of carpenters do side jobs. I wanted to build a pool, do something special, instead of having a perfect back yard."

"The pool has been great. Does Mom know?"

"Not yet. I guess you know that we live paycheck to paycheck most of the time and with Irene going to the community college now and working fewer hours—not your concern. We're going to stop at the gun dealers on the way home. The rifle I left there on consignment hasn't sold. I need to talk to the dealer about lowering the price. Less than what I paid for it but if it sells it will be worth it. It will only take a minute."

I waited in the truck while Dad went in the gun shop. We rode most of the way home without talking.

"I hope this news doesn't spoil Irene's first day at school … Okay. It probably will. How was your first day?"

"Not too bad. Algebra and I probably won't be happy together."

"I know a young lady—"

"Yes. Yes. I thought maybe you could help me. You use math when building things."

"Geometry."

"Davie says it's like putting a motorcycle back together. You just have to figure out how the pieces fit."

"That sounds right. Let me take a look at your book later."

"Is Mom going to go crazy about your citation?"

"Maybe erupt like Mt. Shasta."

When we arrived home, Mom and Allison were in the pool taking turns swimming "laps" which in our small pool consisted of a few strokes, then a flip turn. We watched until Mom climbed out and Allison did a back flip into the water. Then she shot up and down the pool like a dolphin. Mom called out, "Girls only today. There are some cookies on the counter and iced tea in the fridge."

We retreated to the front porch. I felt sorry for my dad. While we waited for the ladies to finish their swim, we talked about football; neither of us were paying much attention.

They came out of the house wrapped in big towels.

"The pool is yours, gentlemen," my mom said. "It's supposed to turn cooler tomorrow. Might be last swim of the season," she added, as Allison slipped by with just a smile and went into her house. Mom continued, "I'm going to change then go next door to help Allison to cook Italian. A little get together to celebrate the first day of school."

"Irene, there's something I want to talk about."

"Later. We'll ring the dinner bell when it's ready." She went into the house. Dad looked relieved.

After we settled at the table and Allison said grace, my dad and Mr. Schultz talked about building and firefighting. The rest of us talked about school. Allison teased me about Ariel. My mother was very excited about attending school. She and Allison talked a little about being the unusual student. Nobody seemed to notice that my dad looked nervous and unhappy.

It was after nine when we got back home. I went to my room and settled down with my history textbook. The house was quiet but not for long. Their arguing voices came through my bedroom wall like it wasn't there. My mother's voice had a sharpness and anger that I seldom heard. My father was pleading for understanding.

"William, you are going to put your fine on the credit card? Not a good idea. I say no."

"What do you want me to do, Irene, rob a bank? It's only until I sell the rifle."

"I knew you would screw it up. This whole 'Saturday morning concrete' deal."

I couldn't stand it. I yelled out "stop!" at the top of my voice.

In the living room, there was immediate silence followed in a few moments by Mom calling out, "Jack?"

I got out of bed and pulled on a robe. I hesitated then opened the door and went into the living room. My mother was crying and my father looked angry and embarrassed.

"Please don't fight," I said. "We knew Dad was taking a chance doing these jobs. We all talked about it. You love the pool, Mom. Give him a break."

"Jack! I can fight my own battles," said Dad.

"It shouldn't be a battle, we're together in this!" I was angry. I was surprised how angry I was. So were my parents.

"William, he's right. We're in this together."

"I want to loan you a hundred out of my savings account, Dad."

My father looked confused. He looked like someone trying to find just the right thing to say. My mother stopped crying. She had a determined look I knew well.

"No, Jack. That is generous of you, but I have three hundred saved. I thought we might spend a weekend in San Francisco, but this is more important, and I do love the pool AND the both of you. I'll pay the fine, William, and you can pay me back when you sell the gun. There, it's settled. Everyone go to bed."

I left them standing in the living room. Even if their conversation wasn't over, I knew they would whisper. To try to get to sleep, I read my history book. Mr. Schultz's motorcycle came down the driveway outside my window. He usually parked in a storage shed at the back of the yard. There was a familiar tapping at my window. I pulled up the shade—Allison!

"Dad and I went for a ride up the mountain road to watch the moon rise over the shoulder of Mt. Shasta. It was great. See you at school tomorrow."

She blew me a kiss and was gone. I went to sleep a happy man.

Chapter Twenty-Two
Skate Park

A week after school started, Allison and I were sitting on our front porch.

"A better skateboard park is not going to happen by itself," she said. "It's great that Doctor Ballard offered to help financially, but we need to go door to door and gather signatures of people who think a skate park is a good idea. A hundred should do it."

"You mean knock on doors?" I said, unable to keep terror out of my voice.

"Jack, they are just ordinary people like us. If we're polite, the worst they can do is say no. Our meeting with the Parks and Recreation board is just two weeks away. Your dad did a good job of drawing plans for bigger ramps, Trevor's parents brought back photos of other skate parks from their trip, so the rest is up to us. Let's face it, unless you're a total beginner or six years old, the park we have now is totally boring."

"No argument there. When are we doing this?"

"A little more enthusiasm would be nice. Tomorrow night after dinner. Okay, a hundred is a lot. Let's shoot for fifty from the area around the park."

We wrote up a speech that focused on skateboarding as a healthy thing for kids to do. We showed people a list of rules: helmets required, no swearing, no loud music, and keep the site clean. People were mostly friendly, but it did take us four nights to gather the signatures. Allison did a great job of presenting our proposal.

My dad volunteered to be in charge of construction volunteers. Trevor's parents gave their positive summary of the skate parks they had visited in other towns. The Parks and Recreation board gave its approval and funding! The park opened a month later. I was surprised how many skateboarders showed up. Allison found some other skateboarding girls to skate with. It felt great to make something important happen. Allison was totally into the whole process. Maybe she'll be a politician someday. *Allison for governor?*

Chapter Twenty-Three
Who Are We?

School. Still mowing lawns. Homework. Allison and I meeting on our front porch after dinner.

"Are you and Trevor the only two eighth graders taking a class at the high school?" I asked.

"Yes, and your point is?"

"Nothing, I just..."

"You're wondering if I like him?"

"I guess."

"His mind is always working. Sometimes talking to him is tiring."

"Has he done that whole 'what would happen if ice were heavier than water' thing?"

"How did you know?"

"I think he does that with everyone. He comes up with science things, I think, when he doesn't know what else to say."

"His collection of animals is impressive, but I don't know, is he just a genius or a genius who is a little off?"

"My mother wonders the same thing. Once after Trevor was over for dinner, she hugged me and told me how glad she was that I was normal. Does normal mean average?"

"I don't think so. Who would want to be average? In the books I read, the main character, which I pretend is me, is never average. I think Trevor might have a girlfriend."

"Who?"

"A ninth grader from his science class. I've seen them in the hallway. I think Trevor is clueless."

"Trevor, Davie and I have been friends for years, but lately it feels like we are—so busy. Davie's the star of the football team, Trevor doesn't climb over our back fence as often as he used to, I don't know."

"Everyone is growing up, moving apart. At least you and your friends are growing up at a normal rate. When my mother died all of a sudden, I had to grow up fast. It sounds bad, I know, but I'm really angry at her for dying. Why couldn't she just have been injured? Then my dad and I could have nursed her back to health. Is that asking too much?"

"I don't know."

"Moving here was a good idea. Back home there were so many things to remind me of her."

"I'm glad you're here."

"Just a few words, but they mean a lot to me, Jack ... Do you sometimes get the feeling that you're not smart enough? I don't mean you personally, too young to understand things, I mean."

"Like your mother's death?"

"Or the lady who lived here before us that you told me about."

"Mrs. Monahan. In a way, I miss her or at least worry about her."

"That's kind of you."

"I didn't tell you this before, but when they took her away and the neighbors were gathered on the lawn across the street applauding ... my mom was there."

"Your mother?"

"Yes. Then she was ashamed."

"I wish you hadn't told me that."

"Part of growing up. Our parents aren't perfect."

"We like to think they have things figured out but maybe they don't. My dad seems unable to relax and just love me."

"I sometimes hear my parents argue about money," Jack said. "Remember the windy day I took you to the tree fort?"

"It was scary. Did I do a good job of pretending to be brave?"

"Sure."

"Liar."

"Wouldn't it be great if you and I could spend a night there—what am I saying?"

"Jack. Jack. That would be so against the rules."

"Just to be away from town, everyone. It's just that we are always being told what to do, everyone has an idea of what we should do, and I don't know, sometimes I dream about running away to Alaska, living in a log cabin, hunting even. I sometimes feel, here in this small town, like I'm wrapped up tight in a blanket! And just over the last year, my friends, and I guess, me, are changing. All those things they talk about in health class."

"Are you unhappy and I haven't noticed?"

"No, not unhappy. Impatient. Worried that I won't succeed. It isn't easy for me to get mostly all A's. And we are not even in high school yet."

"You're smart enough, you work hard, don't worry. I'm mostly happy when I'm with you: making the skate park happen, the rainy day at the library, sitting here now talking. We don't have to figure it all out, like, today."

"I wish we could live more like the Ballards."

"Really?"

"They seem to have their lives set up just how they want them. There's even a rumor that he has sold a screenplay about his motorcycle adventure. They have a real swimming pool. Okay, I sound stupid, it's just that we are supposed to have dreams—all those slogans on the walls at school about being yourself, being a success but we spend all day doing what the teachers tell us to do."

"What is it you want to do instead?"

"Real stuff. Building a house. Skateboarding as good as you. Climbing Mt. Shasta. Baseball. Fighting a forest fire. Go on an African safari. And I don't know, being more honest with people. I feel that some of the time I don't believe half of what I'm saying."

"Not with me!"

"No, with you, I mean everything I say. I even mean things I don't say."

"I know and it's all good, Jack. Enough. Let's go skateboarding."

Chapter Twenty-Four
My Favorite Uncle

When I got home from school the next day, there was a brand-new Ford pick-up with a camper and Alaska plates covered in dust—Uncle Pete! My father's brother. On the back window, in the dirt, he had written, "I drove the Alaska Highway." During the summer, he ran a fishing lodge near Denali Park. During the winter, he was a lodge manager at Squaw Valley Ski Area, California. He had promised to treat me to three days of free skiing "when I was older."

Was I older now? I would have to ride the bus there by myself. I decided not to ask. I had the feeling my mother would say no. She wasn't sure about Uncle Pete, thought he was a bit of a "wild man." Based on his stories, some of which I heard through my bedroom door when he and my dad were in the living room and my mother had had enough of old times and gone to bed, she may have been right!!

Before I could get to the front door, he burst out of the house, picked me up in a bear hug and swung me in a circle. "How are you, buddy boy? You're bigger than last year but are you any smarter?"

"Yes, I am and I'll prove it to you by beating you at chess."

My father called out from the porch, "And he has a girlfriend." Normally, I would be embarrassed by someone saying that but around Uncle Pete I felt proud.

"Beating me at chess will have to wait until after I take you all out to dinner at Shasta's fanciest restaurant."

"Did you bring a coat and tie, you old grizzly bear?" my mother called from the porch.

"I'll clean up, and yes, I have a coat and tie. You never know when you might meet some—"

"No womanizing stories. Save them for your brother later. He's the only one who believes you."

"Fair enough."

"Come on in, everybody and stop cluttering up the front yard," Mom nagged us.

After we got settled in the living room, my father and Uncle Pete each with a beer, I asked, "Did you drive all the way down from Alaska?"

"Put it on the ferry part way. Took a detour through Northern Idaho to see a lady—"

"And probably went down a dirt road just to make the truck dusty," my dad interrupted.

"You bet," Uncle Pete answered.

Whenever the two of them got together, they gave each other a hard time in a loving way. My friends and I did the same.

"It worked. People waved at me all the way down here."

"You bought the truck in Alaska? I thought they were super expensive up there?"

"Normally, that's true. I was playing poker with a car dealer and ended up buying it for dealer cost. He should have quit when he was behind. I won the camper, too. Gave the old truck away to the winter caretakers for the lodge."

"That's your one and only poker story for the visit," Mom warned.

"It's not rightly gambling. I keep a log and year in, year out, I come out about twenty percent to the good. Better than a savings account at the bank. Our grandfather was a great gambler. The boys at the VFW hall would run for the exits when they saw him coming."

"I remember the time he won a horse," Dad said laughing.

"I think the owner lost that horse on purpose. No one could ride him."

"He refused to turn right and was always trying to rub us off on low hanging tree branches," Dad added.

My mom could see where this was going. "If we really are going somewhere fancy, I have first dibs on the bathroom."

"I can shower in the camper then. Sleep there, too."

"Okay. Me, Jack, William. William, I'll iron your good shirt and pants while you are in the shower. Your school clothes will be fine, Jack. I'll call the Green Lantern and make a reservation. Shouldn't be too busy on Monday night."

"Jack. Check out the camper with me."

The camper had everything but looked a little crowded for someone my uncle's size.

"I wouldn't want to live in it, but there is something about moving about with everything you need. Plan to rent it out, on the side, this winter. If you look around, Jack, there is always a way to make money."

"I'm doing okay with my lawns. Next summer, I've been promised a job at the golf course as a caddy."

"Let me know if it happens and we'll have a phone conversation about increasing your tips. And speaking of money," he said, looking back at the house, "hold out your hand like we are going to shake."

I did and when he took my hand, I felt money between our palms. "Put it in your pocket without looking at it. Don't mention it later. This is between us."

When I got back in the house, I looked. A hundred-dollar bill!

At the restaurant, prime ribs all around, Uncle Pete flirted with the waitress, who didn't seem to mind, talked in a loud voice and paid with bills from a money roll in his pocket. My mother did not approve of his behavior. He also talked about how incredible Alaska was: Denali at 20,000 feet, 6,000 feet higher than Shasta, grizzly bears—his stories of close encounters which my mother didn't believe for a minute; about how moose are smarter and more dangerous than they look, and river valleys a hundred miles wide.

And he read my mind. While he was talking about Alaska, a new dream came to me. The dream of going to Alaska and working with Uncle Pete at the lodge when I turned eighteen.

During dessert, Uncle Pete looked directly at Mom and said, "Jack seems a responsible young man. Maybe when he graduates from high school, he can come to Alaska and work for me. Great experience, money for college."

Mom did not look pleased. Uncle Pete backtracked a little. "Famous river guide, Ross McKenna, a straight shooter, and his wife can keep an eye on him." Mom stared him down then went back to her dessert.

The whole time I was thinking that I would be eighteen and could make my own decisions. I didn't want to live like Uncle Pete. It seemed lonely not having a family, but it would be great to have real adventures. That night, I fell asleep to the sound of the two brothers' voices in the living room.

* * *

The next day was a school day. At breakfast, without Uncle Pete who was still asleep in his camper, my father handed me a note, excusing me from the first two hours of school. A mystery that would be answered by Uncle Pete my dad said.

I sat in the living room reading a book and waiting for him to appear. At nine, I went out and knocked on his door.

"Give me a minute." he called out. He stepped out smiling like he had a secret. "Let's get in the truck, Jack."

"Where are we going?"

"To the ski shop for your early birthday present."

I didn't say anything. I didn't want to be disappointed if all I got was a pair of gloves.

Fifteen minutes later, we stood in front of a row of beautiful, brand-new skis listening to the store owner talk about what he thought would be the best skis for me. They were expensive but Uncle Pete didn't seem to care. He did reach an agreement with the owner that changing over the bindings from my old skis would be part of the price.

On the way home, I asked Uncle Pete about the possibility of coming down to Squaw Valley to ski. I had a fantasy of skiing the course that had been used for the Olympic downhill way back when.

"Well, I talked it over with your mother and she said no for now but next year you will be in high school—"

"And old enough to visit you on my own."

"I understand you're buying your own season pass. That's great. So, this year ski the heck out of your new skis and you'll be ready for Squaw Valley."

"Thanks, Uncle Pete."

"You are most welcome. You're a good man, Jack."

Chapter Twenty-Five
Alone in the Woods

Rain in town and the first snow of September on Mt. Shasta was followed by several days of "Indian" summer with warm days and mild nights. Leaves turned color and fell quietly without the aid of wind. A whole day at school seemed like a day wasted. During the last period of the day, I watched two flies buzz against the half-open window unable to figure out how to escape. Even a daydream of riding a motorcycle to Alaska could not shake my gloom. Something had to be done.

My parents had left that morning for Yreka, California, when they heard my mother's sister had been in a serious car accident. They planned to stay overnight. I promised not to have anyone over. She left me meatloaf and a baked potato for dinner. I decided that this was a chance for adventure. A chance to spend the night alone in the woods for the first time.

As soon as school was over, I raced home, took the lawn mower out of the garage, and went down the street to mow the one lawn on my list. When I returned home, I made two meatloaf sandwiches, grabbed the cold baked potato, two water bottles, a package of soup, matches, flashlight, a small cooking pot and a hot chocolate mix. I half-filled a "Maine Guide" backpack my uncle had given me, which I had yet to use, with warm clothes, a sleeping bag and a folding saw. I got my bike from the back porch, looked around the corner of the house to make sure none of the neighbors were out and about, then pedaled like a mad man across town. There was a trail to Hogan's Ridge that started at a city park. I rode my bike up the trail for about a half mile then hid it in the bushes several yards from the trail when the path became too steep to ride.

An hour and a half of hard hiking under the soft light

of early evening brought me to Hogan's Ridge. There was a great view of Mt. Shasta, but I could also see the roof of the county courthouse. I would still be able to see the lights of the town. I wanted to be away from it all. I hiked another half hour east to a second ridge. I found a side trail that ended at a rock outcropping with a flat section guarded by two large boulders with an excellent view to the east. Home!

I cut some cedar boughs for a bed. Gathered small branches for kindling, and using the folding saw, cut some larger branches off a dead tree for a fire I intended to keep going all night. Was I afraid of bears or mountain lions or some maniac? Maybe a little. But overcoming fear was part of being an adventurer. I soon had a small fire going. The darkness settled down. The ground beyond the firelight was soon in shadows. A few bird calls, then silence. Not a sign of human existence. I pulled on my ski jacket, put a pot of soup on to warm, set the baked potato at the edge of the fire, and settled into my sleeping bag.

The first stars appeared in the nearly dark eastern sky. Beyond the light from my fire, I heard the snapping of a twig and the movement of some animal. A doe appeared in the shadows and stood still watching me and the fire. I whistled and she bounded lightly away. I felt light as well. I felt easy. No fear. No loneliness. Not a ripple in the order of things. Star by star the night was born.

I was not sleepy. The stars felt close. Good company. Sweet smell of the cedar boughs that made my bed. The crackle of the fire was the only sound. Peace. I didn't miss the citizens of my town in their houses with the blue television light. I was the adventurer of Oak Street. I was enjoying the comfort of being outside and warm. I had all I needed. Time passed. Stars moved across the sky. I pulled a wool hat out of my backpack and added a few pieces of wood to the fire. I heated a small pot of water to make hot chocolate. It tasted slightly metallic. Delicious.

I watched the stars appear in the east and travel to the western horizon. Time just flowed by. Far sooner than I would have guessed, I saw a hint of turquoise in the eastern sky. I imagined the sun rising out of the Atlantic Ocean. As the darkness faded, I could see the outline of trees and hear the singing of one bird species after another, greeting the new day.

The fire had died to embers. I waited until the sun warmed my sleeping bag, then let myself fall asleep. When I woke up, I was ravenous. I fetched water from a nearby creek, poured it on the embers, stirred and poured again. In what would become a lifelong habit, I thanked the campsite for sheltering me and walked happily out of the woods, not caring that it was a school day and that I would be late for class.

I returned home, showered, changed clothes, and went uptown for breakfast at Lou's restaurant. I ordered the "lumberjack special" and coffee. I took my time eating, left a generous tip then sauntered down to the ol' schoolhouse Tom Sawyer style. I arrived halfway through fourth period. Mr. Hawkins, my English teacher, barely turned from the blackboard to gesture for me to leave my tardy note on his desk. It had not occurred to me to forge one! I had spent the night with millions of stars, why should I care about a note?

I stood by my desk. I was undecided if I should bother to sit down or just walk out of the building. Mr. Hawkins, who had been teaching forever, turned and stared at me. I looked him in the eye.

He saw something. "Oh, never mind, just sit down."

The class stirred uneasily. I could feel Allison staring at me. The girl in front of me turned around and whispered, "How did you get away with that?"

Without answering, I piled several books on my desk, propped open a copy of *The Green Hills of Africa* by Ernest Hemingway and began to read.

As soon as the bell rang, I made for the door. Allison caught up with me.

"Where were you last night? I came by your house after dinner. And this morning? Two hours late to school? And some weird eye contact with Mr. Hawkins? Inquiring minds, mainly mine, want to know. Give it up, Jack."

Put off by how aggressive Allison was being and still, in a way, enjoying the solitude of the woods, I answered her by saying, "All in good time. Trust me." We were outside the door to the shop class. Kids were looking at us. "You'll be late for your music class."

"I expect a full report."

As she walked away, I called out, maybe just to bug her, "I spent the night with God. He let me sleep in."

She kept walking. I felt angry with her without being completely sure why. I guess it wasn't just her, it was the town, the school, everything. I felt I hadn't quite absorbed the lesson of the stars, the joy I had found in solitude. I didn't know how to share with words all I had experienced simply by doing nothing more than lying in a sleeping bag next to a fire and watching the sky go from twilight to darkness to dawn.

Maybe if I wrote it down? During history class, I made some notes. The words were not even close to what I had experienced. When I saw her in the hall later, she asked me to wait outside the school until she got back from her class at the high school next door so we could walk home together. She often walked home with Trevor so that was okay with me.

* * *

"It's hard to explain. I didn't do anything bad. Do you believe me?"

"Of course. Just start from the beginning."

"Okay. There were these two flies buzzing against the window glass."

"Flies?"

"They could not figure out how to escape. I realized I wanted to escape."

"You don't like being inside. I understand that."

I told her the whole story. Well, I told her the bare facts of the story without trying to explain my emotions. She wasn't satisfied but was unsure what questions to ask. I felt bad not being completely open with her. For the first time in my life, I asked the question: If the sky is full of millions of stars and the earth is teeming with life, where did it all come from?

"Maybe when we are older, we can camp out somewhere remote instead of at a campground?" she asked.

"You're missing the point. The point is to be alone. If that sounds selfish, too bad."

"Why are you mad at me? I'm not the one making you go

to school, sleep in a bedroom—sometimes Jack, you remind me of Trevor. Questions. Questions."

"I'm sorry. What I had last night, I want to hold on to it for a while."

"Okay, fine. I thought we were going to share everything, but okay."

We walked the rest of the way home in silence. I thought I might try again to write down the feelings I had during my night alone in the woods.

Chapter Twenty-Six
Escaped Criminal

That Saturday, I sat on our back porch, alone. Two cousins of Allison's, on a cross country camping trip, showed up at her house without warning for a visit, my dad was asked to work overtime, and my mother said she needed to spend time in the college library researching a paper she had to write for her legal secretary class. And my lawn mowing business was tapering off. Bummer!

I was thinking of putting on loud music and cleaning my room when Trevor climbed over the back fence. He saw me and waved. He stopped and looked at our now empty pool.

"We had some good times this summer, didn't we, Jack?"

"And now it's over."

"It's true. The three musketeers aren't spending much time together."

"Yeah, Davie has new friends. Football players and cheerleaders."

"And there is you and Allison."

"True enough. And you and Ruby."

"Hey. Unexpected incoming data. We're just science class buddies."

"Allison says otherwise. Says you're clueless." As soon as I said it, I thought I might have made a mistake. I was right.

"Allison should mind her own business."

"Sorry."

"I came over to ask if you wanted to make a final trip to the tree fort. Last time I was there I saw the bald eagle chase an osprey with a fish until the osprey dropped it. Did you know that eagles, being large and strong, carry fish crosswise in their talons while smaller birds of prey carry them lined up with their bodies?"

"For aerodynamic reasons?"

"Yes. Good thinking. Do you want to ride out to the tree fort? I found a new way to get there, an old logging road, gets us within a half mile."

"Okay. I'll leave a note for Mom in case she gets back early from the library."

"How is she doing in school?"

"Okay. She has trouble memorizing things."

"I know a trick. If you're trying to remember something, look up and to the right."

"Uh, okay. Do rats do that?"

"Good question. I'll watch for it. Have you taken Allison there?"

"I did. The wind was blowing a little. She almost got sick."

"Bummer. I guess you two are serious?"

"As serious as two eighth graders can be."

"Is there any extra food in your fridge? I haven't done the shopping yet this week. We are kind of eating down our supplies."

"That really works for you? Doing the shopping? Cooking your own meals?"

"Yes. Mom and Dad cook sometimes. We made a deal that I got the use of the garage for my science projects, and, in exchange, I shop and cook some. They're busy."

"Don't you get lonely?"

"Sometimes. The basset hound, now that he's older, is better company than he used to be. Follows me around. He and the rabbit have agreed to a truce. My parents and I have time to talk and when we do there are no rules. We can talk about anything: sex, death, money, love, God. You know, everything."

I tried to imagine talking about everything with my parents. I couldn't do it.

"How is the science going? Have you developed a super rat?"

"Not yet, but I have discovered a way to make more time for experiments."

"You haven't cut back on your sleeping?"

"No. I've given up reading fiction."

I was disappointed. For years we had loaned each other fiction and non-fiction books. "Oh, okay. Let's raid the fridge."

* * *

The new way to the tree fort was faster. However, we didn't stay long. Trevor took out his binoculars to check on the eagle, then uttered a cuss word. Something he almost never did.

"What is it? Is the eagle dead or what?"

"Smoke. It looks like it might be coming from our shack!"

"No way. Let me see."

He was right. There was a small column of smoke that just made it above the trees, then vanished. We watched for a minute. It didn't seem to be getting bigger.

"Maybe someone has a cook fire. We should report it," I said.

"No, we should investigate."

I didn't say anything.

"Are you afraid?"

"I just have a bad feeling."

We climbed down. We rode our bikes until Trevor figured we were a quarter mile north of the shack. "Let's leave our bikes here and walk in. No talking."

We started walking. I stopped and grabbed Trevor's arm and pointed to the far side of the clearing. There was something shiny. Out of place. I felt a shiver go up my spine. Trevor looked puzzled. We stood perfectly still, not talking. After a minute, we realized we couldn't stand there forever. We investigated. We found a car that was covered in brush.

Suddenly, we both realized that we might be in danger, that this wasn't a game, that "our" woods had been invaded by someone. Trevor memorized the license plate number. We walked away, retrieved our bikes, and rode like crazy back to town. We stopped at my dad's workplace just as he was packing up to go home. After giving our report, we loaded our bikes in the back of his truck and he drove us to the police station.

The car was stolen. The police arrested a man also wanted

for burglary. When arrested, he was armed. A few days later, on page three of the local paper there was the headline: Local Boys Help Police Nab Car Thief.

Chapter Twenty-Seven
Skipping School

After the excitement of seeing myself in the local newspaper faded, I settled into the routine of going to school, mowing all my lawns every two weeks instead of every week, and helping the Ballards and their gardener extend their Japanese garden. Allison and I spent less time together than we had during the summer. She easily made new friends at school. She had even joined a girl's bowling team one night a week.

Every day before dinner, I did exercises in the backyard to get ready for the ski season. As October faded into November, each time it rained in town, it snowed on Mt. Shasta. I could see the snow line on the mountain moving lower and lower.

On the day after Thanksgiving when we shared a great meal with the Schultz's, it snowed in town for the first time. Just enough that I had to shovel sidewalks. The next day, it snowed a foot and on Sunday, another foot! The ski area announced it would open for the season on Monday, a school day. How could the Fates be so cruel? I had earned enough to buy a season pass and I was eager to try out my new skis.

First thing Monday morning, I called the area's snow phone: twenty-two degrees, no wind, packed powder. Perfect. The three of us ate breakfast without saying much. I think my dad knew what was going on. I think he saw my mother giving me a certain smile. As soon as he left for work, Mom gave me a big smile and said, "Do you want to skip school today? I do."

I couldn't believe she said that, but of course, I said yes. In thirty minutes, we changed clothes, gathered our equipment, borrowed a car from our friends, the Pearsons, and were on our way to the mountain. I was a little sad that Allison wasn't coming with us but excited to have a day with my mom.

There was a carnival atmosphere in the parking lot. Dozens of dedicated skiers and boarders had skipped out on whatever they were supposed to be doing in the valley and driven up to the mountain. Some skiers followed the tradition of wearing funny costumes on opening day. One skier was dressed as a hot dog!

After picking up my season pass and Mom's day pass in the lodge, we joined the happy campers in line at the chairlift. The operators were running the lift to get it warmed up and to send the ski patrol to the top. Right on time, the attendant dropped the rope and yelled, "Let's go skiing!" He was answered by whooping and hollering from everyone in line.

As the chair went higher, we had a view of Shasta's summit. Mom turned to me with an electric smile. "Jack, I am so happy with how things are going for us right now. You're doing well in school, Allison is great, I'm enjoying my classes, your dad will be getting his contractor's license in three months—with jobs already lined up. We are one lucky family!"

"And we skipped school to go skiing! I can't believe it."

"We needed a day together, buddy." She put an arm around my shoulders and gave me a hug.

"Thanks, Mom, for everything."

"You are welcome."

The season before we had skied together just twice and, maybe ten times I had begged a ride to the mountain to ski on my own. My mom skied well. Always in control. Very precise. It all had to do with shifting the weight from one ski to the other at just the right time. When we had skied together the year before, I had mostly followed her down, turning when she did, trying to find that magical rhythm, trying to ski the mountain, instead of the mountain "skiing" me. Mom had pointed out a ski instructor she knew as he took a run on his own under the chair on an expert black diamond run. "He turns where he wants. He is so light on his skis that bumps or changing terrain just don't matter. He's skiing the mountain."

It was beautiful to watch. I wondered if I would ever ski like that. I wondered if people on the chairlift would yell for me as I skied past like we all did for him.

We got off the lift. We tightened our boots. Adjusted our goggles. *Would I remember how to do this?*

"You first Mom."

"Not this year. You take the left; I'll take the right."

The middle of the trail had been packed down by grooming machines. On each side was twelve inches of light powder. We decided to stay on the groomed part for the first few runs. Were we racing? I skated and poled to gain speed on the beginning flat part. I glanced at my mom. She was doing the same. The race was on.

When I went over the lip, I let out a yell. I had forgotten how much fun this was! The mountain, the snow, the brilliant sun, the cold air, the blue sky were all mine! I could tell that my new skis were turning easier than my old pair the winter before—thank you, Uncle Pete! Halfway down I glanced to my right. Mom and I were even. We finished the steep part of the trail and, skiing side by side, making lazy turns, skied together back to the chairlift.

We made some more runs together on the groomed parts of different trails, then decided to take on the powder. It sounded easy enough. We had watched a video: feet closer together, sit back a little so the skis can float, get into an up and down motion, and keep the skis pointed downhill. "Don't ski across the trail, you'll get bogged down trying to turn. Fall down, go boom."

"Okay."

"You have to pick up a little speed," Mom yelled as she took off.

Almost. I almost got the skis to float. I almost got the up and down rhythm. We made three runs. Exhausted, we quit for lunch. We sat on our parkas in the strong sun and ate our sandwiches.

"I need a short nap," said Mom. "I was up late writing a paper."

"Is it okay if I take a run on my own?"

"Sure," she said, pulling her ski cap over her eyes. "Wake me up when you get back."

I stood at the top of Charlie's Chute, a true black diamond trail. It was a short, steep, pitch with a long run out back to the lift. How much trouble could I get in? There was only one way to answer that question. I pointed my skis downhill, took a deep breath, exhaled, and felt gravity take over. I picked up speed quickly. I reminded myself that the steeper the hill, the more forward I had to lean to stay right angled to the slope. I made a turn and immediately moved into the next turn.

A voice in my head kept repeating "you can do this." I refused to be distracted by an image of being hauled off the hill in a toboggan by the ski patrol. My world became small. Ski. That was it. Halfway down I could feel the skis getting steadier under my feet. I was out skiing my fear! The trail turned left then right. I had to turn against the hill. I almost lost my balance but recovered in time to turn to the right, again facing straight downhill. My remaining turns were confident. I had discovered the balance between letting go and yet staying in control. Then I was down.

The rest of the trail was a gentle ride through the trees to meet up with Mom. Gliding through the forest, standing upright on the skis, I took in some oxygen, laughed and shook myself. It was real. I had done it. I couldn't wait to brag to my mom.

She was sound asleep. I shook her shoulder. "Mom, I did it, I skied my first black diamond!"

Without taking the hat off her face, she mumbled, "I thought you might give it a try." Pulling her hat away, she said, "Congratulations. One word of advice. Don't ski the expert trails when you are tired. If your legs aren't doing what you ask them to, time to call it a day or go back to easier trails. Promise?"

"Yes. I promise."

"Okay, buddy. Let's take two more runs on Charlie's Chute, then ease off."

I fell when I was almost at the bottom when I lost my concentration. I remembered my mother's advice and went limp. I bounced once, both skis came off when the safety bindings released. I rolled over a few times. Came to a stop unhurt.

Mom stood over me. "Are you all right?"

"Yes, got overconfident, lost my concentration."

"Do it again, get back on the horse, or ski something easier?"

"Something easier. Actual skiing uses different muscles than workout ones."

"Wait until you're my age. I'm going to call it a day. Why don't you take three more runs and meet me in the lodge."

"Okay."

* * *

The next morning at breakfast, Dad, thinking about us going to school, laughed at our sunburned faces. We looked like raccoons. Our faces were sunburned—all except where our goggles had protected us.

"What are you going to write on his absent note for school? Everyone will know he went skiing."

"I think I will just tell the truth. Something like, 'My son and I had a wonderful time skiing. Please excuse his absence from school.'"

"Sounds good to me," said Dad.

"I thought the three of us might go up together on Saturday," Dad suggested. "It's okay," he added, catching our looks, "You don't have to ski more than a few runs with a slow poke like me."

"That's okay, as long as we ride the chairlift together at least once so we can make out."

I laughed at the look of surprise on Dad's face. Mom got up and ran around the table and gave him a big kiss! Times like this I thought my parents were the greatest.

We did ski that weekend. Allison was able to join us. The two of us crammed into the back of my dad's king cab truck. The four of us skied together for a few runs. Dad took a lot of photographs. Allison skied the black diamonds with me but didn't look happy. After lunch, she and my mom skied together while Dad and I rode the chair together but took different routes to the bottom. For the last few runs, Allison and I skied together. It felt good to be on our own. We hadn't spent much time together lately.

It had been that way since school started. Between her math class at the high school, her bowling team, piano lessons, shopping, and cooking for her dad, plus hanging out with new friends, I felt like I was standing in line to spend time with her. I often took the free bus up to the mountain to ski by myself. I was totally into it while Allison was content to wait for good weather days. The weeks went by until it was spring break. For the first three days of spring break, Allison and I rode the courtesy bus and skied together. Then she left to visit an aunt in Chicago. My mother felt she couldn't afford any more tickets, my dad had skied his two days. I didn't have any friends from school who skied, so I was on my own. That was okay with me. I was completely into skiing.

The edges of my new skis were curved slightly in the length of the ski. When the curved ski was pushed into the snow at an angle, the shape of the ski made the ski turn. When I managed to do it correctly on an intermediate trail, the turn was carved. This means the ski did not slide sideways like in a skidded turn. The feeling of being glued to the mountain was amazing. It also felt like I was accelerating during the turn. Dad paid for a one-hour private lesson to help me reach this goal of carving turns.

"Do you want to drive a Ford Fiesta with loose steering or do you, when you carve, want to feel like you are driving a Porsche?" my instructor, Glen, said.

"Give me a Porsche any day!"

At the end of the lesson Glen asked me if I would be interested in being a junior ski instructor the next season helping teach little kids. "You work two hours a day, get a free pass and a locker in the ski instructors' locker room." I wasn't sure about the little kids part but I told him I would think about it.

The weather that ski season was unpredictable. It seemed that half the time the mountain was fogged in or a blizzard was happening. Besides getting up early enough to ride the shuttle bus, I shoveled the sidewalks for five of my neighbors plus one short driveway. To get it all done on ski or school days I often had to get up at five a.m. Sometimes I liked it.

I liked sipping hot chocolate in the kitchen knowing that when I came home Mom would fix me a big breakfast. I liked the peacefulness of the neighborhood and the way, on stormy days, the snow drifted down through the streetlights. The job would have been harder if Grandpa Hutchins hadn't taken pity and taught me how to shovel.

Grandpa Hutchins was a neighborhood legend. He was seventy-six and still worked every day at his hardware store. He also flew his own plane and rode a motorcycle to work in good weather. He often got up as early as I did to shovel his own driveway. The first time we shared the quiet, pre-dawn street, he watched me work for a while then approached me.

"I'm sorry to bother you, Jack, but when it comes to hard work, I've found there's a wrong way and a right way to do things. Try bending your knees, using your legs to push the shovel forward, then use that momentum and your whole upper body to keep it going. Establish a rhythm. Don't think about how much work it is, just get on with it. You might even discover one of the secrets of good living."

"Would you mind telling me?" I asked, annoyed that I had to be taught how to shovel.

"Work is fun." With that, "grandpa" went back to work. I watched him. He churned through the snow like a snowblower. I decided to copy his style. Sure enough, I moved more snow with less effort. *Would he give me a job at his hardware store when I was older?*

Chapter Twenty-Eight
Surviving the Flood

In town, on the day Allison left, it rained. On the mountain, it snowed, hard. A wet snow that compacted from its own weight into what skiers called "Cascade Concrete" after the mountain range. Snow so heavy and dense it was almost impossible to ski the trails that had not been packed by grooming machines. Unfortunately, on the packed runs, the snow often turned to ice overnight. I wondered if my ski season was over with. I hoped not. I was still struggling to perfect my carved turns. Skiing had become such a big part of my life, I often dreamed about it, that my parents were concerned.

While I was on the lift, the snow turned to rain. By the time I got to the top, it was raining hard. I skied down and joined other unhappy campers abandoning the mountain. It was another hour before the shuttle bus was scheduled to leave. I hitchhiked. I got a ride right away with my gym teacher and his wife. It was a quiet ride down. The rain was blowing across the highway in great sheets.

It rained off and on for the next three days. On the mountain, it rained during the day and snowed at night when the temperature dropped. By morning the new, wet snow was almost ice. By afternoon it, was slush. I stayed home. The next morning when I woke up, I had tossed the covers off. I opened my window. A very warm breeze blew in. If it had been May, it would have made sense, but in March, it was eerie. I checked the thermometer. Fifty-two degrees! Thirty degrees warmer than just a few days before.

At breakfast, from behind the newspaper, my father said "It's supposed to be sunny and warmer than usual for the next four days."

No one seemed to realize that the saturated snow on the mountain was melting at a rapid rate. My parents left for work. I went to the garage, cleaned off a lawn chair and settled down to read on the south side of the garage, wearing my ski jacket. I was still fascinated with Africa. I was reading about early explorers. After lunch, I decided to ride my bike over to Davie's to see what he was up to.

Two blocks from Davie's trailer I heard a rumbling sound that wasn't a train. It sounded like a train, but it also sounded like giant pieces of metal banging together. And it sounded like an angry wind but there wasn't any wind. I wasn't sure what it was, but my body knew enough for the hair on the back of my neck to stand up. I skidded to a stop. Next, I heard the siren of a firetruck on the road behind me. It roared past going toward the river.

The river! The river was flooding! Of course, all that saturated snow was melting. I followed the fire truck to Davie's trailer park. The river was no longer just a river but a rushing wall of water. I turned the corner and the road was underwater. The fire truck was ploughing through. It came up to the chain on my bicycle. I watched as a barn was ripped off its foundation in a twisting motion and torn apart in just seconds.

In what might have been funny on television, a live cow drifted by bellowing! Next a half-submerged car drifted by. If Davie was home, I had to do something. I retreated to an intersection away from the river, followed the railroad tracks until I was even with the trailer park, then turned down an alley. Davie's trailer and one other were gone! The firemen were busy helping a lady from another trailer wade through waist high water to safety.

A pick-up pulled up behind me. It was my dad and another carpenter.

"We were at the lumber yard next to the fire station when we heard about the flash flood. Is Davie's trailer gone?

"Yes, but where is he?" I practically screamed.

"You know the river. Is there a bend or—"

"About a half mile down, there's the old brewery right on the bank. Brick."

"Let's go. I have some safety ropes in the truck. This is Steve. Steve, Jack."

I threw my bike in the back of the truck and climbed

in with it. When we reached the brewery, there were two trailers smashed against it. The building was now midstream instead of on the bank. One of the trailers was Davie's! It was mostly on top of the other one. Davie was at the open doorway.

We had to rescue him, but how? Just then, both trailers shifted. Would the raging river pull them off the side of the brewery building and sweep them downstream? We waved. Davie waved back. Dad yelled as loud as could for Davie to climb onto the roof but at that moment the other trailer broke free and drifted into the main current and was gone. Davie's trailer, which had been end first against the building, turned sideways and rolled a quarter turn. It was pinned against the building but for how long?

Davie was half in, half out of the doorway, facing the sky. He struggled out and tried, without success, to stand on the shaking trailer. We all saw it at the same time—a metal hook that must have been part of a pulley system at one time sticking out of the building above the end of Davie's trailer. We pointed and yelled, "Grab the hook!"

Davie crawled until he was under the hook just as the trailer gave a great shudder. In one athletic movement, he stood, jumped, and grabbed the hook just as the trailer broke loose and sailed away! We cheered and yelled "hang on!" But now what?

"He can't hold on forever," said Steve. "We need to get a rope to him."

"I have a plan," Dad yelled against the sound of the river. "I'll back the truck into the river until the water is just under the floorboards and, Steve, you throw the rope as far as you can and we'll hope it drifts down to Davie."

"That shed looks like it might break loose and smash into the truck," said Steve.

"Right now, it's diverting the strength of the current. Jack. Your job is to watch the shed. Yell if it breaks loose."

Steve tied one end of the rope to the bumper of the truck. He climbed in the back. Dad backed the truck into the river. Steve took a few steps in the bed of the truck and threw the rope. It didn't work. The rope landed too close to our shore. It needed to be thrown another ten feet to be in position to drift down to Davie. If it did reach him, would he have the courage to let go of the hook, fall into the river, and grab the rope?

In the cab of the truck, Dad found a piece of wood. He leaned out the window and handed it to Steve who tied it to the end of the rope to give it more weight.

It worked! The piece of wood, with the rope still attached, drifted downriver to Davie. He looked terrified. I think he had just realized he would have to drop into ice cold water just as the rope reached him. If he hesitated the rope might drift away. The rope hit the wall of the brewery three feet to Davie's right. He had to jump before it drifted away! We were all screaming "JUMP!"

He looked at us as if he might never see us again and jumped. As soon as Dad could tell he was holding the rope, he started to pull slowly forward, hoping to reel Davie in like a huge fish. Just then, the shed I was supposed to be watching broke loose. I yelled and waved my arms. Steve jumped into the water away from the oncoming shed. My dad kept moving at the same slow speed. He was afraid if he went faster Davie would not be able to hold on.

The small shed hit the truck on the side of the bed and kind of half tilted on to it. Dad kept pulling forward. When Davie got to where the water was knee deep, he stood up and started for shore. I couldn't help myself. I ran into the river and put my arm around him to help him to dry land. He was shivering uncontrollably. He couldn't speak but it looked like he was trying to smile.

A crowd had gathered out of nowhere. A large lady in a yellow jogging outfit came forward.

"We need to get him out of those wet clothes. I live just across the street."

Davie followed her. We waited until he reappeared wrapped in a blanket, still looking cold and carrying his clothes in a plastic bag. We hustled him into the cab of the truck and turned on the heater full blast. I climbed in beside him. Steve climbed in the back.

Davie finally said something. "We lost everything."

"We'll take you to our house. Jack's clothes will fit you."

Just then we saw Davie's dad driving toward us. Both trucks stopped. Davie's dad jumped out and ran over.

"Thank God you're safe!"

"I'm sorry I didn't save the motorcycle. It all happened so fast."

"That's okay. We have insurance for losing things, but not on losing you!"

"Let's go to our house. Figure something out. I'll drop Steve off at the job site," suggested Dad.

When we pulled into the driveway and got out, Mom dashed out of the house and hugged Davie, joined by his dad.

After Davie disentangled himself, he said, "I'm okay. I just need a hot shower and a strong cup of coffee."

I don't know why but we all started laughing!

"Coffees all around and there's apple pie. Everyone inside."

While Davie was in the shower, we decided that he and his dad would move in with us for a few days. Davie and I would camp out in the backyard in a tent while his dad could have my room. They had insurance, but to lose everything from a toothbrush to schoolbooks meant it would take time to get back to normal.

The river was back in its banks after three days. Two elderly sisters who lived in the trailer next to Davie's had drowned. They were the only fatalities. Davie and his dad moved into a motel after spending five days with us and a few months later, using the insurance money, bought another trailer in another park on the far side of town well away from any river.

Life returned to normal. Davie went out for the track team. He never talked about the flood and how he almost drowned. Trevor won a Science Fair award. He spent the prize money on a very powerful microscope and for the next week ignored everyone as he dove into the world of microscopic bugs. He told me he was going to discover a cure for diabetes. His mother was diabetic and he worried about her. The ski season ended. Allison and I were still together. No more shoveling sidewalks. The grass was growing and would soon need mowing. The town of Shasta on planet earth seemed like a good place to live.

Chapter Twenty-Nine
Building a Boat

A few Saturdays after the end of the ski season, Davie showed up my house.

"I've something in the woods I want to show you. Let's go for a bike ride."

"Are you going to tell me what it is?"

"No."

We rode our bikes in the direction of the shack and continued past the golf course.

We turned off, stopped at a rusty metal gate across an abandoned road, climbed over and kept riding, dodging in and out of small pines like we were in a ski race. A mile in we stopped at another closed gate. On a nearby tree, there was a rusted sign decorated with bullet holes. It read: Keep Out. Property of Bulldog Logging.

"I asked my dad about it," Davie said. "They went out of business twenty years ago. The county took over the property. No one cares that we're here."

The gate was locked. We climbed over and rode for another ten minutes and came to a clearing. All that was left of a large sawmill was a few concrete pads overgrown with weeds and a tumbledown shed.

"You hauled me all the way out here to show me this?" I demanded. "How did you find it?"

"My dad and I found it mushroom hunting last fall. And we found this," he said, leading me around to the back of the shed.

"Okay," I said. "It's a pile of old lumber, so what?"

Davie took a hand plane out of his pack and smoothed the first two feet of one of the boards. It was beautiful, straight grained, not a single knot.

"Cedar," I said. "Again, so what?"

"Yes. Cedar. If they are all straight grained like the one I planed off, then we are in luck."

"We? Are we going to haul it off on our bikes and sell it?"

"Wrong question. Close your eyes and imagine what we might build with this wood."

"A boat?"

"What kind of boat?"

"Oh, I don't know. How long are the boards?"

"I brought a tape measure ... fourteen feet."

"Okay. A fourteen-foot day sailer," I said.

"With a cockpit big enough for a guy and his girlfriend. Are you more interested now?"

"Maybe. How are we going to get the materials to our non-existent boat shop?"

"Later. Check this out," Davie said, going into the shed and pulling an old tarp off a very heavy-looking band saw. "A band saw. Just what every boat builder needs."

"It looks like it weighs a ton. We'll never get it home."

"Not to worry. There's another road in. Too far to ride on our bikes but my dad agreed to come out with his truck to help us."

"Not to be a 'doubting Thomas' but how are we going to lift it into the truck?"

"An inclined plane, just like they used to build the pyramids. We build a ramp, put the saw on a furniture dolly and roll it up the inclined plane."

"And haul it where?"

"Dad rented a storage shed. There's some room. We'll store it and the wood there until we work something out. Trust me, Jack. I love to build things. If we can build a boat, we can build anything. This book will help us. Like Trevor says, 'You can learn anything from a book.' "

Davie held up the book: *Build a Sailboat— A Guide for the Beginning Boat Builder.*

"I found it at a used bookstore. I had almost forgotten about this pile of lumber."

"I almost wish you had."

"Jack. We've outgrown your fantasy adventures. Time for something more challenging than the tree fort."

"Okay, I'm in," I said while thinking of Allison and me sailing together. I opened the book. It had been published in 1947. There were pictures of complicated looking forms on sawhorses, a list of materials, and a drawing of the side of the boat showing how to apply the lapstrake siding.

"Do you think we'll need Trevor to help with the math?" I said. "If we can pry him away from his new microscope."

"I guess. I'll show him the book and bet him that he can't figure it out."

"That should do it."

"I know what you are thinking. You're wondering if deep down building a boat has something to do with almost drowning. It doesn't. I haven't talked about the flood much. I have nightmares once in a while. I feel bad about my neighbors drowning. I wonder if I could have done something to save them. It doesn't matter that it was a flood. It only matters that I survived with the help of my friends. 'Life is precious' my aunt used to say. After nearly drowning, I know what she meant. So, I'm not afraid of water. I just like to build things."

"I always wondered how you found the courage to let go of the hook and fall into the river?"

"Courage had nothing to do with it. I couldn't hang on any longer. That was then. Back to work. Here's the material list. We have the cedar for the hull and there's a scrap pile with what I think is fir and some pieces of metal that might be useful. I'll do the measuring and you write things down."

Chapter Thirty
A New Friend

When I got home, I went next door to tell Allison about our boat building project. She wasn't home. She was probably visiting her new friend, Celeste, I thought. Allison had answered a classified ad offering piano lessons in exchange for some light housekeeping. Celeste was a retired schoolteacher who, with her husband, had retired when they had inherited her uncle's small farm just outside of town. The next year, her husband had died. Allison told me that Celeste was legally blind. She had an Australian shepherd to keep her company. Allison did one hour of housekeeping and reading the mail in exchange for a one-hour piano lesson. Lately she had been going out twice a week.

"She wants to meet you," Allison said when she came over after dinner to help me with my algebra homework. My dad had long ago lost interest in being my tutor.

"Why?"

"I've told her about you."

"Why?"

"Are you nervous about talking with someone who is blind?"

"Of course not."

"Then ride out there with me tomorrow. She's great, traveled all over the world, has done crazy things like sky diving and spending a summer in an ashram in India."

"Okay. If that's what it takes—"

"Bad attitude, Jack."

"Okay. Okay."

"She's not completely blind. She can see shapes as if she was swimming under the surface of murky water."

I closed my eyes almost all the way but couldn't really picture it.

"She told me about this narrow river in Alaska. Some winters the lake that feeds the river completely freezes and the surface of the river freezes. The rest of the river drains leaving a dry bed with a ceiling of ice. Can you imagine?"

"You can walk around under the ice? Sounds great but what does it have to do with her eyesight?"

"She says looking through the ice, wavy images, is how she sees the world. She makes these ... creative connections when she talks. My grandma used to do that."

"I can see it. The magical river."

"Mostly she talks and I listen. She and her husband, he was a schoolteacher, traveled every summer. Over the years, they visited over twenty countries and did stuff like hiking in Nepal, rafting the Grand Canyon, and hiking the Pacific Crest Trail."

"Wait a minute! That's my future life we're talking about."

"Closer to home she has climbed Shasta five times and Mount Rainier once."

"I have got to meet this lady. When are you going to see her again?"

"Tomorrow."

"Count me in."

* * *

The next day after school, we rode our bikes to Celeste's house. When we pulled into the driveway, we could hear a piano being played. Allison said, "You have to pass the 'Charlie test.'" Before I could ask what the "Charlie test" consisted of, a barking Australian Shepherd came around the corner of the house. It stopped in front of us and looked at me.

"This is the test. Don't make doggie talk. If he goes to the porch and lies down, then you've passed."

"What happens if I fail?" I whispered.

"I would probably never speak to you again."

Fortunately, Charlie gave one short bark and went to the porch. As we got off our bikes, Allison told me he was a one-person dog and not to pet him. The piano went silent, and Celeste came out on the porch.

"Is that you, Allison?"

"Yes."

"Have you brought someone with you?"

"Yes. Jack."

"Welcome, Jack. Come on in. I baked some biscuits this morning."

Under the watchful eye of Charlie, Allison hugged Celeste, then stepped aside so we could shake hands. Celeste held onto my hand for several seconds as if she could learn something about me. I wasn't sure how to look at a blind person. *Should I look directly at her?*

"It's okay to look at me," Celeste said. Her eyes looked cloudy and gray. I think they were once blue. We went into the kitchen. Celeste explained that Allison had made labels for different ingredients in large, black letters. "I can read them if I hold them up close in a strong light. There are four dinners I can make plus some baking."

We sat down to biscuits with real maple syrup, iced tea, and the best cheese I had ever eaten.

"Fancy cheese is one of my sins," Celeste said with a laugh. "I add a different variety to my grocery order every week."

I didn't know what to say. I was amazed how Celeste had adapted to her condition. Allison cleared the table. "Tell me about your boat building project. It sounds difficult. How do you measure all those curved pieces in a boat?"

"We have a 'how to book' and we have a team—"

"But you need shop space?"

"Yes," I said, glancing at Allison who pretended to be busy with the dishes.

"Let's take a walk."

We stepped outside. Charlie joined us. I could tell he was working. He mostly stayed between Celeste and me. Always on the alert.

"It's so nice of Allison to bring her young man to meet me. I can tell you respect each other. That's important."

"Yes, ma'am."

"I rent out the barn to my neighbor for equipment storage. His burned down. But here's a possibility. When my uncle owned this farm, he had a small dairy herd. This was the spring house and refrigerator. Ten by twenty feet. A little tight but it should be big enough. Open the door and I'll explain."

The building was made of stone. The heavy wood door had sagged on its hinges, but I managed to get it open.

"Take my arm Jack, help me inside. I can't really see what's at my feet."

I did so. The stone walls of the building were two feet thick. There were no windows. Down the middle of the stone floor was a channel about a foot deep and two feet wide.

"Water from the spring was directed to the channel, then flowed out and on to the vegetable garden. Milk and food in metal cans was placed in the channel to stay cool."

"No electric bills."

"True. I'm planning to run electricity over from the barn. After you finish your boat and set sail, I'm thinking of using it as a pottery workshop. You're forewarned, you might get a coffee mug for Christmas," she added laughing.

"Here's the deal. I have a roofer coming to fix the roof. You convince your dad to help build a plywood floor and install ceiling joists so we can insulate. An adult has to run the table saw and the band saw but you and your friends, with your parents' permission can use handsaws and a small saber saw. I'm trusting you and your friends are sane enough to be safe. What do you think?"

"I think this is something I really want to do."

"Good. Challenges are what make life worth living. Allison's dad invited me for dinner tomorrow. I expect all parents to be there."

"Yes, ma'am."

"Let's go inside."

While Allison was finishing her housework, I called Davie's and Trevor's houses. All promised to come to dinner the next night. When it was time for Allison's piano lesson, I hauled in firewood.

"I like an evening fire even if I don't really need it," Celeste said.

Next, I sat in the far corner of the living room and looked through a scrapbook of Celeste and her husband's adventures. The collection included articles Celeste had published in various newspapers and magazines. I felt lucky to have made a new friend.

* * *

Two weeks after my first visit with Celeste, we had completed the repairs to the shed. We were ready to become boat builders. We had a pile of lumber and three "how to books." We checked two more boat building books out of the town library.

"You can learn anything from a book," Trevor reminded us, but he didn't sound that positive. The problem was, while the framework for a house is straight and corners are ninety degrees, in a boat everything is curved. Other than running power saws, we were determined to do the rest of the work ourselves. The day I brought home "The Book," I stared at the drawings for so long I saw them in my sleep.

Trevor came to the rescue. He cleared off the workbench in his garage and we built a two-foot model of our boat out of balsa wood. Trial and error and error and victory. Finally, our model looked just like the boat in our book.

"The two hardest parts of a project are the beginning and the ending," my dad reminded us. "Most carpenters dream of building a boat and never get around to it. You guys are doing it."

Our boat was still a pile of lumber. We hung our model from the ceiling for inspiration. We had trouble deciding who was in charge but after a while Davie became the job foreman. He loved being in the shop. Step by step like it said in the book. We decided to name the boat Celeste. The way she coped with her near blindness, the way she was learning to read Braille, her sunny attitude—we just loved her. Maybe I was a little jealous of the close relationship between her and Allison but that was okay.

Sometimes life goes as planned. The boat took shape. We all worked on Saturdays. Celeste didn't allow us to work on

Sundays. Every Wednesday, Allison and I, and sometimes Davie, would ride our bikes out after school. I worked while Allison did chores and took her piano lesson. Celeste, again bearing cookies and a hot chocolate, asked me if we had found all the materials we needed. I told her we had everything except something to make the mast.

"Finish your snack. I think it's great the way the different families are all behind your efforts."

"Allison's dad has offered to teach us how to sail. He was an instructor at a summer camp when he was in college."

"I bet I could learn. I can see big shapes."

"You are now officially a member of the Lemurian Yacht Club."

"Thanks. Let's walk to the barn."

I liked it when she slipped her arm in mine. When we stepped inside the barn, Celeste took a deep breath. "Hay, dust, manure, it's such a warm, comfortable smell. Is there still an old wagon tongue hanging from the rafters?"

"Yes."

"Does it look long enough for your mast?"

"Yes."

"It's yours. I like the idea of it having a new life on the lake."

* * *

In six weeks, the boat was finished except for sanding and painting. Celeste insisted on doing the sanding. With her sensitive fingertips, she could tell when the boards were smooth. We decided to have a party to christen the boat. We invited our parents. Davie's dad did a barbecue. It felt like family. The Lemurian Yacht Club was born.

Our first order of business was the unveiling. I escorted Celeste into the shop. She ran her hands over the trim lines of the boat. When she traced the raised letters on the stern and realized it was her name, she was overwhelmed. Blind eyes can cry.

The next weekend, the entire boat club gathered for our first lesson. Mr. Schulz and Celeste went out first. He later told me that she seemed to be able to feel the wind in the sail, the motion of the boat, when to pull in the sail, when to let it out, better than a sighted person.

When they returned to shore, she was radiant. "I haven't had that much fun in ages."

We did rock, paper, scissors to see who went next. I won. It was great. When we were just the right angle to the wind and the boat surged forward—nothing like it. The boat was great. It didn't fall apart and sink.

While Davie took his lesson, Trevor explained Bernoulli's principle to me. "Have you ever wondered why an airplane lifts off the ground? Or a sailboat can sail across the wind?"

"Now I wonder."

"The engines on a plane make it go forward but what makes it lift off the runway?"

"If you're waiting for an answer, it could be a long wait. Okay. Magic."

"Suction."

"Of course, that explains it."

"The bottom of the wing is flat and the top is curved. Air travels faster over the top of the wing than the bottom. So ..."

"It's thinner. And the plane is sucked upward. It doesn't seem possible. I may never fly again."

"Understandable. My parents have a friend who is a pilot, he says he is surprised every time he takes off successfully. And with our sailboat?"

"You are making me think way too hard for a Saturday. Okay. When the sail fills with wind, it is curved just like the airplane wing. Our boat is getting sucked down the lake."

"Not now. Now they are sailing with the wind but to get back they will have to come about and sail at a diagonal to the wind. Being sucked along. When they get near the shore, they will tack, or come about, so by zigzagging, they will get back to the dock. Might take them some time if the wind dies down."

* * *

The Lemurian Yacht Club, with Celeste as secretary arranging who would sail and when, became a summer long success. We didn't mind sharing with adults. Besides we needed someone to drive us to the marina where we kept "Celeste." The parents had chipped in to pay for the slip.

Allison and I sailed together at least once a week when she was in town. Mom and Celeste often teamed up. Davie and his dad preferred to sail on really windy days. Trevor's parents lost interest and dropped out. Trevor followed their example. Once a week, Mom would drive Allison and me down to the marina where we kept Celeste. While we sailed, taking turns at being captain, she would sit in a lawn chair and read. It was a quiet time for us.

Chapter Thirty-One
Do We Dare?

My mother is extremely goal oriented. I had no doubts that she would complete her classes at the community college and get a job as a legal secretary. My dad quitting smoking was due as much to my mother's nagging as to his own will power. When she decided, at the beginning of seventh grade, that I would get all A's and B's, it was a done deal. There was just no way I was going to bring home a report card with a "C" on it. Two months before the last day of school, she had announced that she and I were going to climb Mt. Shasta. She would continue her workouts at the college gym and, six days of the week, I would ride my bike over to the high school and run up and down the stadium steps.

"You did say you wanted to climb it."

"When I was older."

"Some consider Shasta to be an active volcano. Maybe it will blow up and we'll miss our chance."

"I doubt it. What about Dad?"

"He'll be our support team."

"What if I say no?"

"I'll be disappointed, and you will disappoint yourself. Just imagine standing on the top."

I did. *If I wanted to be an adventurer, why not start with the imposing mountain right in our backyard?*

"Okay. I'm in. I guess I have some leftover ski muscles. How many times do I have to run up the stadium steps?"

"I leave that up to you. Let you define your limits."

"Thanks. Fourteen thousand, one hundred and sixty-five feet."

"Only if we start at sea level. Actual climbing?"

"About 4,500 feet," I answered."

"We can do this," Mom said.

"To the top," I shouted. It became our rallying cry.

* * *

The challenge of mountain climbing is simple: how to get from base camp to the summit and return without dying, being injured, or causing the death or injury of a fellow climber. Climbing Mt. Shasta required the use of an ice axe and crampons. An ice axe looks like a lightweight pickaxe with a head consisting of a blade and spike. The blade is used for cutting steps in the snow on steep terrain and the spike, driven into the ice, can keep you from falling off the mountain. Crampons are metal contraptions with spikes that you strap on the bottom of your boots. You can walk on steep ice fields by stamping the points into the ice with each step.

Fortunately, we had an expert mountain climber living just up the street—Doctor Ballard. He agreed to loan us the equipment and took us on a training session. On the mountain road, on a north facing slope, he found a short, steep pitch of hard pack snow good for our lesson. It wasn't a rainy day, but he told us to wear rain gear. We soon found out why.

The biggest worry for a beginning climber is losing one's footing and sliding down hill. How to put on the brakes? Doctor Ballard had us wear rain gear so we would pick up speed when we practiced self-arrest. He wanted our training to be like the real thing. First, we learned what not to do. From just twenty feet up the hill, he told me to fall on my back. Wearing the slippery rain gear, I immediately picked up speed.

I dug in my feet to stop. My feet stopped but my body did not! Quicker than I could think about it, I had flipped over my feet and was sliding face down! This would not be good on a big mountain. How to stop? Doctor Ballard demonstrated. As soon as he started to slide, he rolled over, drove his ice ax into the snow and put his weight on it.

"After you stop or self-arrest, pull your knees up and kick the front points of your crampons into the snow, slowly stand up and resume climbing."

"Whoa," I said to myself. *We aren't just walking uphill a month from now, we're going to be climbing a MOUNTAIN.* I looked over at Mom. She looked worried.

"Practice," Doctor Ballard said. "Ten times."

Then we practiced climbing. We were instructed to drive each foot on every step, then lean forward almost as if falling while bringing the other foot forward. Next: establish a breathing rhythm by exhaling with force. Next: descending, especially on rocks. Lean forward so your weight is on the front of your foot.

Two hours later, Doctor Ballard announced we had passed the class. I wasn't sure if I felt more enthusiastic about climbing "our" mountain or less.

"A final word. If you don't trust your partner, don't go."

My mother and I looked at each other. "To the top," she said.

"To the top!" I answered.

Chapter Thirty-Two
Other Plans

The morning after school was out for the summer, Mom invited Allison over for a celebration breakfast of pancakes topped with ice cream. After breakfast, Allison and I rode our bikes to the skateboard park. We stopped at a vacant lot where there was a good view of Mt. Shasta. The snow-covered summit was shining bright.

"By ten tomorrow morning, I'll be on top," I said, trying to sound confident.

"I'm proud of you, Jack."

"I haven't climbed it yet. I'm worried I won't make it."

"Just don't take any unnecessary risks."

"Everyone is expecting me to make it."

"Your mother wouldn't let you go if she didn't believe in you."

"All these years of looking up at the mountain, it's what makes our town special."

"Climbing it won't change that. Maybe next year you can climb it and ski down."

"Whoa."

"Maybe next year we can climb it together? ... Jack?"

"Sorry. For a minute, I was picturing the whole climb, all at once. Tomorrow I'll be looking down."

"I'll wave."

"There's something you want to say, I can tell. We had a good year, didn't we? The two of us, I mean."

"We had a great year! I just found out last night, another girl changed her mind. I've been hired to be a junior counselor at a camp in Colorado for handicapped kids. I'm leaving the day after tomorrow. I'll miss you. I'll be away a month."

"Well, yeah, okay. That's great. We'll both be busy, I guess."

"You'll be fine. I'm more worried about my dad. I'll be gone on the anniversary of my mom's passing."

Neither of us knew what to say next. We went to the skateboard park which was packed with kids celebrating the beginning of summer vacation.

Chapter Thirty-Three
To the Top

In the late afternoon that same day, we parked my dad's truck at a parking lot on the Mountain Road at seven thousand feet and climbed three thousand feet to our bivouac at what was called Lake Helen even though there is no lake there, just small ponds of snow melt among scattered boulders at the base of a headwall. Our plan was to get up at first light and reach the summit four hours later.

The headwall, the steepest part of the climb, faces mostly south. The summer sun turns it into a giant solar collector. There are rocks embedded in the ice at the top of the wall. Loosened by the sun, they sometimes come hurtling down the mountain. Over the years, climbers have been killed and injured. The quicker we could summit and return to where Dad would be waiting, the safer we would be.

I liked the weight of the pack on my shoulders. I liked how strong my legs felt. I almost couldn't believe that I was climbing a 14,000-foot-high mountain! We did have to stop several times for my father to catch his breath. He had stopped smoking several months before, but his lungs were not strong.

At Lake Helen, climbers over the years have cleared "flat" spots among the rocks for places to sleep. We were crammed into a space barely six by eight feet. After a spaghetti dinner cooked by Dad over a small camp stove, he read us some Alaska poems by Robert Service while we watched the sunset. There were maybe a dozen other climbers hunkered down for the night, some in colorful tents, others, like us, in the open. Unlike state campgrounds, it was quiet, no loud voices, no radios. The mountain was quiet and so were we.

Doctor Ballard had loaned us three heavy-duty sleeping bags. Dad fell asleep as soon as it was dark. He gently snored. Mom and I looked up at the stars.

"I can't sleep," I whispered.

"I can't either," she said. "I have never seen so many stars."

I thought of telling her about the time I snuck off to the woods and slept alone but decided not to. I didn't want to spoil the moment.

"Here comes the moon," my mother said.

A sliver of light had appeared on the shoulder of the mountain. We watched in silence. The full moon seemed to balance on the edge of the ridge, then float into the sky. The light was strong enough to read by.

"We better get some sleep," she said. "Big day tomorrow."

I could feel the cold outside my bag where it belonged. I fell asleep thinking about how wonderful it was to be on the mountain and woke to the smell of coffee. Dad was crouched in the rocks nearby heating water for instant coffee over a small camp stove. Lights shone in some of the tents.

"Good morning," he whispered.

"Good morning," I responded. "Thanks for coming with us."

"Glad to be here."

He shook Mom awake and handed her a cup. He gave us each a bowl of granola, cheese, apple slices, and a sliced banana smeared with honey.

I held up my cup. "To the top!"

"To the top!" they answered.

We took up our packs as soon as there was enough light to hike safely. "A journey of a thousand miles begins with a single step." An hour later each step seemed harder than the one before. And it was harder to take in oxygen. Above ten thousand feet, the amount of oxygen in the air is the same as sea level, but the pressure is less which makes it harder to fill your lungs. Trevor had explained this to me earlier but knowing it didn't really help.

My mother called out, "We need to find a rhythm in our breathing."

We had both forgotten Doctor Ballard's advice. We started breathing out forcefully which forced us to inhale completely. We sounded like steam engines. It worked but I still had questions: would my legs give out without warning? If I couldn't keep up, would Mom go on without me? As I climbed, I tried to enjoy being on the mountain despite the pain. And I told myself how proud my parents would be, how impressed Allison would be, and how it would be when I bragged to my friends that I had made it.

Finally, we reached a break in the headwall called Red Rocks. Above there, Doctor Ballard had assured us, the climbing would be easier. I hoped he was right. My legs were starting to scream. When we reached the snow field above the rocks, Mom called a break. We were in full sunlight. The reflection off the snow was blinding. As we had practiced, I stood below her, turned sideways and braced my foot against hers. She took off a layer of clothing, put on sunglasses, drank some Gatorade, and ate a power bar. I carefully stepped around her. She braced my foot and I repeated the routine.

"The air is so thin. Do you want to turn back?" she asked me.

"No!" I answered. It was the strongest "no" in my life.

"To the top?"

"Yes!"

We marched on. Heat became a factor. Three of our four small bottles of water were empty. We packed snow into the empty bottles. Two climbers, who had already made the summit, passed us going down. They said something encouraging but I guessed they didn't think we would make it. I was determined to prove them wrong. One step at a time.

I called out to my mother, "If I can't make it, I want you to go on without me." It was a lie.

She pretended not to hear me. We stopped again. We finished off the Gatorade. We marched on.

When we reached the final, nearly flat snowfield, we could see the rocky spire that was the true summit. We were going to make it. We walked side by side. I had never felt so close to my mother. We were always a team, but this was a team of equals.

A light wind carried the smell of sulfur from a hot spring on the far side of the snowfield. It reminded me that we were climbing a volcano. Naturalist John Muir once spent the night next to the springs to keep from freezing to death when he stayed too late on the mountain to climb down.

That morning, I had felt the weight of the mountain looming above me. Now I felt the mountain holding me up. I looked north. I imagined climbing each of the big Cascade mountains in order: McLoughlin, Hood, Rainier, and Baker. Then on to the mountains of Canada and Alaska. Denali: 20,000 vertical feet.

My legs almost gave out. I tried not to, but I stopped.

"Jack. It's only about two hundred steps more. Let's do this together. I take a step; you take a step. Ready?"

I nodded glumly. It seemed impossible. My mother put her arm around my waist. We moved.

One hundred and seventy-five to go. Don't stop. Suddenly, I felt a new strength flowing into me. I shook my mother off and walked on, almost leaving her behind. We passed the sulfur springs, trying not to breathe in the noxious fumes.

We made it! We hugged. We laughed. Two other climbers arrived. We took their photo. They took ours. I inhaled the cool, sweet mountain air. I looked at my climbing partner. There were tears in her eyes. I looked out at the world.

"How do you feel?" she asked.

"I feel big ... and humble ... older than this morning. I feel great!"

"Me too, but I'm a little worried about going down."

"Just remember what Doctor Ballard said about leaning forward and putting your weight on the front of the foot."

"The snow will be softer this time of day."

"Watch for rocks!" We said in unison.

"Dad will be able to see us when we get below Red Rocks. He's promised a lunch of hamburgers, potato salad, and a coke."

"Really?"

"Really."

I took a few minutes to look at the world from the four compass points. What I saw was freedom. I had chosen to climb this mountain and when I turned eighteen, I could choose my life even if some of my choices might be different from what my parents might choose for me. I wasn't sure if I wanted to go to college. I looked north. I felt Alaska calling me. I felt strongly that climbing this mountain was as important to who I was as sleeping alone in the woods had been the year before. The phrase: "An outdoor life," went through my mind.

"Did you say something?" my mother asked.

"All this," I said sweeping the horizons with my arms, "is bigger than I imagined."

"Yes, it's wonderful. I'm glad we got to share it."

More climbers arrived. We started down. The same upper thigh muscles that got us up the mountain would now be our brakes. I expected them to burn. I wasn't disappointed. When we passed Red Rocks, we had the steep bowl to descend to where my father was waiting. Was that him? Mom untied her bright red parka from her pack and waved it. The tiny figure below waved back with an American flag which we had forgotten to take with us. *Next time.*

After the promised lunch, we packed up and started down the easy trail to the parking lot. I had the strangest feeling of leaving something behind. Would it be waiting for me the next time I climbed a mountain? When we neared the parking lot, I slowed down and let my parents get ahead of me. I looked out at Northern California and holding up my arms, called out, "Look out world. Here I come!"

About the Author

Warren Carlson grew up in a small college town in New Hampshire. His parents didn't worry about Warren or his siblings. They roamed the town, the college, and woods east of town. And yet, Warren felt constrained, so he went to college at the University of California, Santa Barbara. After graduation, Warren and his wife raised two boys in a small, college town in southern Oregon. His childhood and his sons' childhoods were the inspiration for this book. Many of the stories are true, or nearly true, while some are imagined.

When Warren was in the fourth grade, his teacher read a story of his to the class. Before she finished reading, he had decided to be a writer. Warren is intrigued by the process of writing, especially when something totally unexpected appears on the screen.

Warren has visited forty states, worked in national parks, climbed mountains, volunteered at an orphanage in Tanzania, taught English in Azerbaijan as a Peace Corps Volunteer, and still the challenge of the blank page is his favorite adventure.

To the Top! Adventures of a Small Town Boy is a prequel to *A Boy A Bike Alaska!* also published by Fathom Publishing.

www.ingramcontent.com/pod-product-compliance
Lightning Source LLC
Chambersburg PA
CBHW070045260626
47159CB00005B/2129